When Love Wins

Sherryl D. Hancock

Thanks for reading!

Sheryl D. Hancock

Originally self-published by Sherryl D. Hancock 2016

Published by Vulpine Press in the United Kingdom 2017

ISBN 978-1-910780-18-3

Cover by Armend Meha

Cover photo credit: Tirzah D. Hancock

www.vulpine-press.com

ACKNOWLEDGEMENTS

Thanks to Google and the fantastic websites that the Air Force has online. Thanks to the men and women of the armed forces who lived under the cloud of Don't Ask, Don't Tell and made it through the other side.

To my love, my life, my soul mate, the person that made writing this story possible. I love you Tirzah, thank you for loving me and giving me everything I never realized I needed.

CHAPTER 1

"So you're gay," Shenin Devereaux said, her tone matter of fact.

"Yep," Tyler Hancock confirmed simply, her brow furrowed. She couldn't tell if Shenin was freaking out, or if she didn't think it was a big deal.

Shenin and Tyler had been friends for six months. They were both airmen in the United States Air Force, and part of the same unit at Nellis Air Force Base in Las Vegas, Nevada. They belonged to the security force detail on base, and were responsible for on base security, policing activities for Air Force personnel, as well as anti-terrorism.

They'd first met on the day Shenin arrived at the base. She'd been transferred from Beale Air Force Base in Sacramento, California. She'd just checked in with the base commander, but hadn't been told where the barracks for the base were. She'd been standing outside, trying to decide whether or not to just wait for someone to walk by who she could ask, or go back inside and ask. That's when a person on a blue Harley Davidson motorcycle pulled up in front of the admin building.

Shenin watched as the person, definitely a woman, got off the bike. She took in the jeans, cowboy boots, leather chaps and blue and black Harley Davidson jacket, it looked warm, she was freezing, since she was wearing a short-sleeved uniform, and hadn't thought to grab her jacket out of her duffel. She also noticed the long braid that went down the woman's back almost to her waist. When the woman turned around and took off the helmet, she smiled and Shenin saw the deepest dimples she'd ever seen, with a very bright smile and very blue eyes.

Tyler couldn't help but notice Shenin. For one, she was a redhead, and she also had a body that would stop the proverbial Mack truck. There was no way she was going to avoid talking to this one, no way in Hell. Shenin made it easy.

"Is that a Softail?" Shenin asked, looking at Tyler's bike.

"Heritage," Tyler said, nodding, then quirked an eyebrow. "You ride?"

"Yeah," Shenin said, nodding and smiling, "not a hog though."

"What do you have?" Tyler asked.

"Honda Shadow Spirit 750," Shenin replied.

"750?" Tyler repeated, looking surprised, thinking that she might need to re-evaluate the new comer, "impressive."

"Yeah, yeah, I know," Shenin said her tone wry, the look on her face mocking as she said, "little thing like you, with all that power between your legs..." Her voice trailed off suggestively, like most men's would after a statement like that.

Tyler laughed, nodding. "Yeah, I've heard shit like that more times than I can count."

"Annoying as fuck, isn't it?" Shenin said, rolling her eyes.

"You said it!" Tyler agreed.

They both laughed.

"We should ride sometime," Tyler said, smiling.

"That would be great, just not when I'm going to freeze my ass off," Shenin said, shivering.

"Or dying of heat stroke," Tyler added.

"Or that," Shenin said, nodding.

"Senior Airman Tyler Hancock," Tyler said, extending her hand to the other woman.

"Airman 1st Class Shenin Deveraux," Shenin replied, shaking Tyler's hand.

"So where are you headed?" Tyler asked, having noted that Shenin looked lost when she pulled up.

"Women's barracks, security force."

Tyler looked momentarily surprised, then nodded. "You must be the newbie we've been expecting," she said, grinning.

"Four damned years in, and I'm the newbie again, son of a…" Shenin replied, her voice trailing off.

Tyler laughed. "Don't worry, we're not all bad," she said, grinning. "You're actually going to be bunking with me; we're two and two in the dorms. Welcome to Nellis," she said, smiling. "So where you are from?" Tyler asked.

"Beale Air Force Base," Shenin said.

"California?" Tyler replied.

"Land of fruits and nuts," Shenin replied, having heard it before.

"I like fruits and nuts," Tyler replied winking. "Look give me a few minutes, I'm headed to the barracks anyway, I can take you there."

"That would be great!" Shenin replied, "I waited on the flight line at Beale all morning, and now I finally get here and it's friggin' cold, and I just want a hot shower and some shut eye."

"I think that can be arranged," Tyler said, smiling, "just give me a few."

Shenin nodded, and watched as Tyler strode into the building.

Ten minutes later, Tyler came out of the building and noted that no less than five guys were buzzing around Shenin, trying to engage her in conversation, two of them were officers. Tyler stood back watching, she noticed that while Shenin was answering questions, and being what appeared to be polite, she didn't seem to be taking advantage of her looks. There was no hair twirling, no batting of eyelashes, nothing like that; she was simply standing there talking to the guys. She certainly didn't seem to have any guile or game, Tyler found that she immediately liked that about the girl.

When Shenin saw that Tyler had come out, she politely excused herself, nodding in acknowledgement to the two officers. The men, however, seemed loathe to let her walk away. Shenin glanced back at Tyler and Tyler got the silent mayday immediately.

Walking over to the group, Tyler acknowledged the officers with eye contact and a respectful nod; she didn't need to salute because she wasn't in uniform.

"Okay, boys," Tyler said, moving between the men and getting to Shenin, her grin sly, "back off, security force property here." And with that, she took Shenin's arm and guided her away from the men, bending down to scoop up Shenin's duffel while she walked by and guided the younger woman to her bike. The men looked on as Tyler gave Shenin her helmet, climbing onto the bike, and Shenin climbed on behind her. Tyler placed Shenin's duffle over the gas tank of the bike, and started the engine with its legendary growl and rumble. Winking rakishly at the guys, she gunned the engine and expertly turned it to drive off.

As they rode toward the barracks Shenin found herself huddling behind Tyler's five seven" frame, because it was cold. Part of the ride got bumpy, and Shenin gripped Tyler's jacket at the waist, Tyler grinned at the feeling. It was the beginning of their friendship.

Six months later found them arriving at Ronald Regan National Airport on leave. Tyler had invited Shenin home with her. They made an interesting pair, Shenin being smaller, and such a contrast to Tyler in many ways. Tyler's hair was long, golden brown, and extremely curly, she had a slim but strong build, whereas Shenin was petite, but curvy, with silky straight rich auburn colored hair, that hung a couple inches past her shoulders. Tyler dressed in simple jeans, her customary black cowboy boots, a button up shirt and leather Harley jacket. Shenin was dressed in black slacks, a mint green tank top with a long light black jacket and dress boots on her feet. Tyler wore no make-up; Shenin not only wore make-up but jewelry that was color coordinated with her outfit as well. They were very much opposites.

As they left the baggage claim, Tyler bent down to pick up her camera backpack, and loop it over one shoulder, she also picked Shenin's laptop case, looping it over the other shoulder.

"I could have gotten that," Shenin said, giving her friend a narrowed look.

"Now you don't have to," Tyler said, grinning.

Shenin shook her head, Tyler was forever doing things like that, so she was getting used to it, but she never wanted to assume that Tyler would always do it for her.

As they walked out of the airport to catch the bus to the rental cars, Shenin was shocked by the way that hot, damp air struck her almost physically. Automatically she started fanning herself with her hand.

Tyler noticed Shenin's movement and grinned.

"Welcome to Maryland in the summer," she said, rolling her eyes as she did.

An hour later they were in their rental car on the way to Tyler's family home, when Tyler's cell phone rang, the display on the Bluetooth connection on the car displayed the name "Angie". Tyler answered the phone with her customary answer when she knew the person.

"What're you doin'?" she asked, smiling.

"Where are you?" Angie replied sharply.

Tyler blinked, obviously surprised by either the tone of the voice, or the question, or both.

"I'm, uh, home," she replied, "in Maryland."

"Sheila said you took Devereaux home with you, is that true?" Angie asked her tone hurt.

Tyler glanced over at Shenin, already regretting the hands free Bluetooth in the rental car.

"Yeah, she's with me," Tyler said, her tone of voice taking on an edge that Shenin easily recognized as her way of cautioning the other person to be careful with what they said. Apparently "Angie" either didn't recognize the tone, or she decided to ignore it.

"Are you fucking her, Tyler?" she screeched into the phone.

Tyler instantly snatched up her cell phone, canceling the hands free, and holding the phone to her ear. "Have you completely lost your mind?" Tyler practically growled, "or have you just decided that Don't Ask, Don't Tell no longer applies to me or the Air Force?"

As Tyler listened to the woman on the other end of the line, her look was passive, but Shenin been able to see that her eyes were turning to ice, slowly but surely as the woman obviously ranted on and on. It didn't appear that Tyler was fazed by anything the woman was saying. When the woman went silent for a long minute, Tyler calmly asked, "Are you finished?" her voice was as cold as the icy look in her eyes.

Shenin could hear a short and meek sounding reply.

Tyler nodded, "I will be back in ten days, have my stuff packed, I'll pick it up when I get in."

With that she hung up the phone and calmly set it down in the cup holder of the car. Shenin kept silent, not sure what she could possibly say after that conversation. She was decidedly shocked by what she'd just heard, although looking at it in hindsight, she also realized she should have really figured it out. She also knew that discussing it with Tyler at that point wouldn't be the right time or place, and she didn't want to upset Tyler anymore.

Once the tension in the car finally eased, Shenin made a point of asking about other things like the houses, or the signs, allowing Tyler to have her privacy at that point in time.

Tyler was greatly relieved that Shenin hadn't jumped on the gay thing right away. Tyler needed time to figure out what she was going to do.

Don't Ask, Don't Tell had been brought in to lift a ban on homosexuals in the military. It essentially said that the military shouldn't ask military personnel about whether or not they were gay. The bill had also included a part about "don't pursue, don't harass." Military personnel knew it was bullshit, and in no way shape or form truly protected gay members of the military from persecution. It put gays further into the closet, because they could not talk about being gay, or engage in any sexual activity. It was a ridiculous bill that only served to further alienate gays in the military. It was a joke that gays were told they couldn't engage in sexual activity when their heterosexual counterparts could have sex with any member of the opposite sex every minute of every day, and twice on Sundays if they so desired.

The idea that Don't Ask, Don't Tell, allowed gays to be open with their sexuality was complete and utter bullshit, and no member of the military, gay or straight thought any differently.

It was Don't Ask, Don't Tell that struck fear into the hearts of any gay service members. It was a gag order, a death sentence to your career, it was no protection at all and it didn't stop the military from dishonorably discharging gay service members. The fact was that the discharge of gay and lesbian service members had increased steadily since the law was enacted in 1993. It was not a good time to be gay in the military, and Tyler knew that full well. She had not gone into the military knowing that she was gay, but she was also not willing to lose her career over something she felt was none of the government's business.

Being gay had shredded Tyler's home life when she'd come out to her parents. She'd always been a daddy's girl, and had, indeed joined the branch of the armed forces that she had because her father was retired Air Force. When she'd discovered she was gay two years into her service, she'd known that it was going to devastate her parents, and likely her large family. It hadn't been an easy thing to deal with, and it still wasn't.

Growing up in Port Tobacco, Maryland, Tyler hadn't really been exposed to anyone who was gay. She'd been a tomboy, but then again, so was her mother, and she wasn't gay. Her parents had been happily married for over thirty-five years. For Tyler, being back in her hometown always seemed strange, ever since she'd left over twelve years before. Getting out into the world had opened her eyes to many things, being gay was just one of those things. The trip back to

Maryland had been the first in five years, the first since she'd finally admitted to her parents that she was gay.

By the time Shenin and Tyler had reached her parents' house, Shenin had decided to wait to talk to Tyler about the phone call. She easily sensed, from what she knew about Tyler's relationship with her parents that the gay thing was probably not well accepted. The last thing Shenin wanted to do was to upset Tyler right as she was seeing her parents again. The house they pulled up to was a red brick construction with wood framed windows painted white to match the front door. It was an older ranch style home, with a carport and long driveway. Tyler's parents came out of the house to greet them. After a fairly awkward round of hugs, Tyler introduced them to Shenin.

"Mom, dad, this is Shenin, she's a friend of mine from Nellis, we're on the security force together. Shenin, these are my parents, Carl and Becky."

"It's nice to meet you," Shenin said, smiling and extending her hand to each of them. "Your daughter was my very first friend at Nellis." Her smile was so warm and genuine that Carl and Becky couldn't help but like her right away.

"Tyler always did make friends easy," Becky said, smiling at her daughter.

Shenin looked between them, and wondered how much her parents knew, and how much damage had been done to their relationship if they did know.

Finding out their only daughter was gay had been jarring for Carl and Becky. Tyler had always been a tomboy, but she'd also dated guys in high school. She'd even been engaged, before she'd decided to enlist in the Air Force. They just couldn't comprehend what had happened to change her so drastically and they still weren't sure how to deal with her. What they did know was that they loved their daughter and that they would do their best to understand her life choices.

Tyler easily read the resolve on her parents' faces, they were trying to cope, and she couldn't help the little flame of hope that started in her heart. They meant the world to her, and knowing that she'd disappointed them or made them ashamed of her, broke her heart every time she thought about it. Sometimes Tyler didn't think she could handle facing them, but she'd known she needed to. Her father had been having heart problems, and the last thing she wanted was for the last memory she had of him to be their last conversation. She'd told him that she'd had the realization that she was gay; his response was to tell her she needed to stop hanging out with whoever she was hanging out with, that they were being a bad influence on her and would get her thrown out of the Air Force. Her mother had shaken her head in disgust and said, "You're just letting people tell you that kind of garbage, it's not true." They hadn't understood, and at the time, they hadn't tried to understand, at least not as far as she was concerned. She'd left that same night and hadn't gone back for five years, this was the first time since then.

The memory of that last visit had been so clear that when she'd told them she was coming home, and they'd insisted that she stay with them, she'd been fairly sure the priest who'd given her first communion would be there to greet her. Her other thought was that they'd kidnap her and take her to a deprogrammer so they could get her unbrainwashed from that gay cult she'd joined in the desert. Neither seemed to be the case at the moment, but she knew it wasn't impossible that there'd be a dinner or two with the local clergy.

"So you're Air Force?" Carl asked Shenin, his look skeptical.

"Yes sir," Shenin replied. "Airman first class."

Carl nodded, then looked at his daughter. "You make sergeant yet?" he asked.

"Not yet, dad, but I'm working on it." Tyler told him, making him smile.

He looked at Shenin again. "So you're on the security force with Tyler?" he asked, again skeptical.

"Yes sir," she said.

"Little thing like you?" he said, sounding very old fashioned suddenly.

"Yep," Shenin said, holding back a grin. She could see that he wanted to say something about little girls carrying big guns, or something like it. She'd heard it for years now.

She knew it always shocked people that someone as small as her, at five four and a hundred-thirty pounds could be in the security force. She actually liked that it shocked people; she liked being more than a pretty face. She knew that sometimes it made her a target too, and that was why she'd become lethal in hand-to-hand combat, with a black belt in karate, and an expert with weapons. Shenin Devereaux could protect herself.

"Well, come on in," Becky said, gesturing for them to go inside. "It's awfully muggy out here."

"Tyler, I put you two in your old room, on your old trundle bed," Becky said, leading them down the hallway of the house.

Tyler grinned. "Thanks mom," she said.

"Go ahead and get unpacked, dinner's in an hour." With that Becky left them to unpack.

Two hours later they had eaten and retired to Tyler's old room. That's when the conversation started...

"So you're gay," Shenin said, her tone matter of fact.

They were lying in the bedroom Tyler had lived in when she was growing up. They were sleeping on the trundle bed she'd had sleepovers with her friends on years before. Tyler was on the upper part of the bed, while Shenin was on the lower 'drawer'. There were a lot of pictures of Tyler growing up, and it was obvious she was not only a tomboy, but also a daddy's girl. Her father had coached her softball team when Tyler was much younger. There were lots of pictures of Tyler and her dad as she grew up. There were also pictures of Tyler with guys that she'd gone to prom and junior prom with. It was pictures like that Shenin was thinking of when she asked the question.

"Yep," Tyler confirmed simply, her brow furrowed. She couldn't tell if Shenin was freaking out, or if she didn't think it was a big deal.

"Not sure why I didn't see it," Shenin said.

"You feel like you should have?"

"Yeah," Shenin said.

"Why? Because you're from California?" Tyler asked, grinning.

Shenin laughed, hearing how dumb it sounded. "Well, we are the land of the fruits and nuts," she said, grinning. "Location of gay mecca, right?"

"What, San Francisco?"

"Yep," Shenin said.

"Never been there," Tyler said.

"Oh," Shenin replied, slightly deflated, "honestly though, I should have sensed it better. How good of a friend am I if you've felt like you needed to hide it all this time?"

"Honestly, Shen," Tyler said, settling on her side to look down at her friend, "I just didn't want to mess things up with us."

"What do you mean? Did I seem like someone that wouldn't like you if you were gay?" Shenin asked, worried that was the case.

"Shen, if I didn't think you'd like the real me, I wouldn't be able to be friends with you," Tyler said. "But you never know with people, especially other members of the security force… you know?"

Shenin thought about that for a minute, then nodded. "Yeah, I guess you'd need to be careful until you were sure you could trust a person not to out you."

"You got that right," Tyler said.

"I'm not going to out you, Ty," Shenin said. "I hope you know that."

Tyler blew her breath out. "Yeah, I guess I do know that."

"You didn't mean for me to find out, did you?" Shenin asked then.

"I didn't mean for you to find out that way," Tyler corrected. "I was going to tell you, probably on this trip. I just wasn't ready for you to find out that way."

"So Angie is someone you're dating?" Shenin asked.

"Was dating," Tyler said, emphasizing the word "was."

"That must be scary," Shenin said, "having someone like that just put your business right out there with no idea who was in the car with you, or what they knew about you."

"Yep, and it's not something I can forgive. Jealousy is one thing; stupidity and endangering my career are completely different."

They were both silent for a moment, Tyler was thanking her lucky stars to have such an understanding friend, it had been a concern that Shenin would pull the whole regulations angle, and say she had to report it. Shenin was pretty forthright when it came to regulations, they were, after all, the law on base.

"So, you're really okay with this?" Tyler asked, with that last thought in mind.

"Tyler," Shenin said, looking a little surprised, "you're assuming I've ever agreed with Don't Ask, Don't Tell. It's complete bullshit, and anyone that believes that it's okay to treat people like that is dumber than shit, and not someone I ever want to associate with. I get that it's a regulation and all, but it's a dumb fucking regulation and not one I'm ever going to hold with, I don't care what it costs me."

Tyler's eyes widened at the outburst. "Tell me how you really feel, Shenin, don't hold back," she said, grinning widely, even as her eyes shone with a glazing of tears for someone truly being on her side. This girl was one in a million, it was too damned bad she was straight.

Shenin smiled, not commenting on the tears in her friends eyes, but touched by it all the same.

"This must have been so hard on you," Shenin said, reaching up to touch Tyler's hand. "With them," she said, indicating Tyler's parents sleeping in the next room.

"Oh yeah," Tyler said, blowing her breath out. "They were really shocked, it was hard on everyone."

"Including you," Shenin put in.

"Yeah," Tyler said, "this is the first time I've been home in five years."

"Oh, Ty…" Shenin said, squeezing her friend's hand, "I'm so sorry you went through that. It's not right the way this world treats people that don't fit some crazy idea of 'normal,' but you have to know that they love you. I could see that tonight."

"I know they love me," Tyler said, "but they're having a hard time understanding this aspect of my life."

"Give them, time, Ty." Shenin said.

"I know," Tyler said, sighing, "I just worry about my dad."

"I get that," Shenin said, nodding.

Again they were quiet for a while each lost in their thoughts.

"Are there others?" Shenin asked.

"That are gay?" Tyler asked.

"Yeah, in the squadron I mean," Shenin said.

"What do you think?" Tyler asked.

"You want to test my gaydar?" Shenin asked.

"Well, it failed you on me, obviously," Tyler said, grinning.

"Yeah, but it's not really a surprise to me either, I really think it was just not important to me what sex you preferred. You're my friend, and that's all that's important to me."

Tyler nodded, still astounded at how easy this had ended up being; there hadn't been an awkward strange moment between them.

"So, who?" Tyler asked, prodding her friend.

Shenin narrowed her eyes for a minute, "Well, Terri, definitely."

She named their lieutenant, who was very butch, and also a really great team leader and everyone in the unit had the utmost respect for her.

"Too easy," Tyler said dismissively.

"Okay..." Shenin said, narrowing her eyes again, then looked at Tyler again. "Jean," she said, naming another member of the unit.

Tyler smiled, nodding. "And the last?"

"That's harder," Shenin said, but then when she thought about it, it really wasn't, they were the two women, that seemed to totally get Tyler. "Sheila."

"You are good, Sheila is very stealth," Tyler said.

"It has nothing to do with her," Shenin said. "It has to do with you; the three of you seemed to totally get each other. I originally chocked it up to your time together in the unit, but now I know that's not the only thing."

Tyler nodded, again, Shenin seemed to grasp even the most subtle things about her and her lifestyle.

"Hey…" Shenin said then, her tone suspicious, "now I totally get that whole toaster joke between the three of you," she said, her eyes narrowed.

Tyler started to laugh. "Oh, no, don't include me in that, I'm just a bystander."

"So how does that joke go again?" Shenin asked.

"Well, we don't really spell it out, usually, but for you, I'll make an exception." Tyler said, winking. "Basically if a lesbian can recruit a straight woman to the life, they get a free toaster."

"And here I thought they were being nice to me," Shenin said, making a face. "Bitches!" she exclaimed, laughing.

"Nah, they like you, they just think you're hot, too."

"I see," Shenin said, grinning.

Tyler grew quiet for a moment, reaching down, she took Shenin's hand in hers, and squeezed it gently. "Thank you for this," she said sincerely.

Shenin smiled softly. "Always for you," she said her tone strong.

The next few days were spent visiting Tyler's old haunts and meeting her family. Tyler had a lot of family; Shenin ended up feeling like Tyler was related to at least half of Maryland. It was interesting to Shenin that none of Tyler's family seemed to have any problem with her being gay, in fact many of them seemed happy to accept the idea that Shenin was her partner. Tyler had to explain over and over that Shenin was just a friend. The more time Tyler spent around her family, the more comfortable she became, it warmed Shenin's heart to see it in her friend.

One night, three days into their visit, they were eating in a local restaurant having dinner, just the two of them. Tyler suddenly stopped talking and was staring just over Shenin's shoulder. Shenin glanced over her shoulder and saw a man standing there his eyes fixed on Tyler. He looked around the same age as Tyler, maybe a couple of years older, but it didn't seem that time had been as good to him as it had been to Tyler.

"Jason," Tyler said, nodding to the man that had once been her fiancé.

"I heard you were in town," the man said, stepping toward the table, his eyes going to Shenin. She noted the hostility in them. So did Tyler.

Tyler was on her feet instantly, putting herself closer to Shenin. Shenin could sense Tyler's tension and recognized her defensive move to protect her.

"Yeah, I'm here to visit my family," Tyler said.

"Guess you weren't brave enough to face me though, huh?" he asked, his tone snide.

Tyler took a long pause, letting her eyes travel from his thinning hair, past the beer belly to his dirty tennis shoes then back up to his face.

"I don't see what I'd have to fear from seeing you," she said, her tone calm.

"You fucked me over, Tyler," he snapped, gesturing toward Shenin with a dismissive wave. "For that."

Tyler glanced behind her at Shenin, her blue eyes sparkling with barely contained malice. "That," she repeated to Shenin, her tone flat and sardonic, then she looked back at Jason. "That," she said again, her head nodding back toward Shenin, "could take you apart with her bare hands, so I don't think you want to fuck with her. As for what you think I did to you, get over it, it was years ago."

Jason looked stunned, this wasn't the easy going Tyler he used to know. She was harder, it had to be the gay thing. Being gay made women hard like men. Besides, that's what they all wanted, to be anyway, right?

"You lesbians are all the same," he sneered, glad that people were now staring at them. "You all just wish you were men."

Tyler grinned, having heard that one often enough. "No, dumbass," she said, her voice calm. "It's men we're trying to avoid, that's the whole point."

"Fucking dyke!" Jason exclaimed, reaching out to shove Tyler, a move she easily dodged, grabbing his arm and wheeling around to wind it up behind his back, wrenching it upward, making him stand on his toes. It was a move she'd used a lot on drunken airmen, and they were usually in much better shape than Jason was.

Shenin stood up, stepping over to Jason and leaning in.

"You might not want to call her that," she said, her tone conversational, "she doesn't like it and she might just break that oversized chicken wing of yours." She smiled sweetly, her look belying her words.

Tyler patted Jason on the shoulder with her other hand, "So why don't you run along now, so I don't have to plant your face on the floor. Okay, sweetie?"

With that she let him go, giving him a shove that had him stumbling to keep from ending up on the ground. Jason quickly left. Tyler looked around the restaurant that had grown silent and still during the incident. She noted a number of nods and approving looks.

"Sorry for the disruption folks, but boys will be boys," she said, wryly, sitting down as Shenin did the same.

There was laughter from a few patrons, and even a little bit of applause.

"Well, that was fun," Shenin said, grinning, as they resumed their meal.

"Sorry, about that," Tyler said looking chagrinned.

"You can't help how other people act," Shenin said.

"No," Tyler said, "but I'm sorry that my baggage is piling up near you."

"Ty," Shenin said, reaching her hand out to touch Tyler's, "I'm never going to stand by while a man acts like that toward any woman, let alone my best friend."

Tyler smiled. "Even if it gets you splashed with gay paint?"

Shenin narrowed her eyes slightly. "There are much worse things to get splashed with, like bigoted mini penis paint for one."

That had Tyler laughing out loud, nearly snorting soda up her nose as she did.

"Seriously, though," Tyler said, her look direct, "thank you for that."

Shenin shrugged, shaking her head. "Just backing my partner's play," she said.

It was a simple statement, but it spoke volumes to Tyler. She knew in that moment that her faith and trust in this woman was well placed. Shenin could have easily have been very put out, even angry about being involved in this kind of scene, and to be assumed to be gay as well. But none of that seemed to bother Shenin, she'd been there for her friend, no hesitation, no questions asked. It was amazing. Tyler was finding out all the time that the world was filled with amazing people.

The rest of the trip was less dramatic, and before long it was time to leave. They'd enjoyed their stay, visiting historic places such as the Dr. Samuel Mudd house, as well as touring some of the museums and veteran monuments in Washington, D.C.

As Tyler said good bye to her parents, her father hugged her for an extra moment.

"We love you," he told her. "We just want you to be happy," he said then, bringing tears to Tyler's eyes as she nodded, unable to speak for a moment.

"I love you guys too," she finally managed.

Shenin looked on, happy for her friend, and knowing that it was what Tyler had needed to hear.

Later on the plane, while Tyler slept, Shenin reflected on the trip. She'd learned a lot about her friend in the past ten days. She'd learned that her best friend was gay. She'd also finally been able to assign the appropriate word for the way Tyler was so often: gallant. It described actions like picking up things for other women and it also described the instinctual reaction Tyler had when she'd intervened between Jason and her. Tyler was gallant, like the knights in medieval days, or the cowboys. That thought made Shenin grin; Tyler lived in her favorite cowboy boots when she wasn't on duty and when it wasn't hotter than Hell outside. She was also known to wear a cowboy hat on occasion. It was endlessly ironic to Shenin. What she did know was that her friend was an incredible person, and she was very happy to be associated with her.

CHAPTER 2

Tyler's gallant streak was further proven a week later when the first major thunderstorm rolled through the Las Vegas desert. They were both getting ready to go out on Friday night when the first bolt of lightning streaked through the sky. The subsequent crack of thunder had Shenin letting out a yelp from the other room.

"Shen?" Tyler queried from the bathroom, as she tried to tame her curls long enough to pull them up out of her face. "What's up?" she asked.

When she got no reply she walked out of the bathroom into their room. "Is it another spider? 'Cause if it is, I'm not gonna put it out in this rain... storm," she said, her voice trailing off as she saw that Shenin was sitting on her bunk shaking from head to toe.

"What the..." Tyler began, just as another bolt of lightning lit up the dorm room window and she saw Shenin jump in reaction.

Tyler strode over to her roommate, dropping to a knee in front of her, and reaching up to take Shenin's hand in hers. She noted they were like ice.

"You don't like thunderstorms?" Tyler surmised.

"Is that what they're supposed to be? They don't usually sound like that in Sacramento," Shenin said.

"Well, that's what we call them here," Tyler said, grinning, making Shenin grin too. She then moved to sit on the bed next to Shenin, and hugged the girl to her side. "They don't usually last long around here," she assured the smaller girl.

Shenin didn't say anything, she just buried her head in Tyler's curls, shuddering as another crack of thunder fired off.

"It's okay," Tyler soothed, not sure what else to do.

They stayed that way for ten more minutes, while the thunderstorm blew itself out. During that time, Shenin's hands once again found their way to the waist of Tyler's shirt, gripping it by two handfuls. The thought that it felt really good to her, pricked the back of Tyler's consciousness, but she refused to look at it too closely.

"So," Tyler said, trying to break the tension. "You come here often?" she said, grinning again.

Shenin grinned, but just shook her head, her forehead still pressed against Tyler's shoulder. Tyler gave Shenin a little squeeze, just to remind her she was there.

When the storm finally seemed have passed, Shenin sat back, letting go of Tyler's shirt. The momentary disappointment Tyler felt also got filed away in the back of her mind.

"You okay?" Tyler asked, looking down into Shenin's eyes.

"Yes," Shenin said, nodding. "Thank you," she said, looking apologetic.

“Just backing my partner’s play,” Tyler replied, mimicking the words Shenin had used back in Maryland after the Jason incident, her way of pointing out the huge difference in the two situations.

Shenin smiled. “Smart ass,” she muttered.

“You know that,” Tyler replied.

With that, they got up and continued to get ready to go out. Later that night at the club Tyler found herself watching Shenin, it surprised her that the little powerhouse had a small weakness. What amazed her more was that Shenin had allowed her to see that and was open enough to let her help. It warmed Tyler’s heart even more toward the petite little redhead.

The rains that summer caused a lot of flooding in Clark County. The US Air Force at Nellis was asked to help in any way they could. The security force was asked to help protect flooded homes from looters, and watch for people trying to get back into their homes, when the situation was dangerous. Tyler, Shenin and two other members of the team, Sheila and Jean, were all assigned to an area. Sheila and Jean were two of Tyler’s best friends in the Air Force. Sheila, an outspoken and sometimes outrageous brunette, was forever putting Tyler in some kind of crazy situation she’d have to talk her way out of, but she was a good friend. Jean was a much quieter and unassuming person. Also a brunette with short hair, Jean more represented the “butch” lesbian stereotype, she was also a good friend, fortunately less troublesome than Sheila.

After a full day of rescuing people from their flooded homes, and ensuring the safe passage of others trying to evacuate, the team was tired. They were in two different Humvees, Tyler was driving in the lead vehicle, with Shenin riding in the passenger seat, an M-16 held across her chest, her eyes looking around them watching for any trouble. Sheila drove the second vehicle, with Jean riding shotgun.

"Got movement up on the right," came Sheila's voice over the radio.

Tyler reached up and activated the mic on her shoulder. "Got it," she said. Then to Shenin she said, "You see anything?"

Shenin looked through the scope of her rifle, using the night vision. "Yep, got 'em, at two o'clock."

Tyler turned the vehicle in that direction, even as she spoke into the mic again.

"Looks like we're gonna get wet," she said, to Sheila. "Maintain cover."

"Ten-four," came the instant reply.

Pulling the vehicle to a stop Tyler glanced over at Shenin, catching her eye and nodding. They got out of the vehicle on either side, Tyler drawing her sidearm as she did. As Tyler came around the vehicle, a shot rang out and she was sure her heart stopped.

"Shenin?" she yelled, as she crouched in front of the vehicle. When there was no answer at first, her pulse kicked into overdrive. "Devereaux answer up!" she ordered.

"Yeah," came Shenin's voice, sounding weak. "I'm here; it came out of the house on the left there!"

"Are you hit?" Tyler called.

"I'm fine," was the immediate reply.

"Unit 2," Tyler spoke in the mic, "move in, we're taking fire!"

"Already here, boss!" came the reply as a shot rang out from behind them. Tyler was relieved to hear the report of an M-16 rifle.

Cautiously she moved from her position to get around the vehicle. She was stunned when the first thing she saw was the scarlet stain against the blue camo fatigues Shenin wore. "I'm fine," Shenin reported, weakly.

"Son of a bitch!" Tyler growled as another shot fired off from the house. She immediately lunged forward putting herself between the direction the shots were coming from, and Shenin who was leaning heavily against the Humvee. She began firing as she strode toward the house. She heard and felt, rather than saw, that Sheila was doing the same with the M-16. Glancing behind her, Tyler saw that Jean was moving to get Shenin behind the Humvee.

Within a minute, Tyler had kicked in the door to the house, and with Sheila's help, moved through it to a back bedroom. Tyler ran headlong into it, weapon at the ready. The man at the window wheeled on her, but Tyler was so mad she literally slapped the weapon out of the man's hand.

"This is my house!" he yelled, even as he threw his hands up in the air. "I was protecting my house!"

"You shot a United States Airman you fucking idiot! We're the good guys!" Tyler screamed at him.

"Oh!" the man exclaimed, obviously shocked.

"I got this," Sheila said from behind Tyler, moving to intercede before Tyler wrung the man's neck. "Go check on Dev."

It took Tyler a moment to control the urge to beat the shit out of the man, but then she nodded, and turned to leave. She made her way through the house, her boots sloshing in the foot of water on the floor.

Tyler got back to the Humvee, her focus solely on Shenin who still sat leaning against the vehicle while Jean assessed her condition.

"She was hit in the shoulder," she said, then canted her head to the side. "Looks like you took one too, Hancock," she said.

Tyler started to disagree, but when she looked down at her sleeve, she saw blood on her forearm. She suddenly realized that it did indeed hurt; the adrenaline was keeping the major part of the pain at bay, apparently.

"I'm fine," Tyler said, her tone sharp. "I'll get her back to base. You go help Sheila," she ordered.

"You got it," Jean responded instantly, sensing that this wasn't the time to argue with Tyler about driving while she was injured. She liked her head where it was.

Tyler bent down to help Jean get Shenin in the vehicle. Shenin was now out cold. Gritting her teeth against the panic that kept wanting to climb up her throat, Tyler got into the driver's seat and brought the engine to life with a roar, throwing it into gear and speeding off toward the base.

Tyler really wanted to believe it was the blood she'd lost that made her want to pass out when the doctors at the Air Force hospital approached with news on Shenin. She really did. It would be so much easier if that had been the problem. Lack of proper blood pressure is a perfectly acceptable reason for a hardened security force airman to pass out. However, passing out because you were terrified that the doctors were about to tell you that your best friend was dead, was not. Definitely not in what would be considered a combat situation. She'd never make sergeant at that rate.

"Airman Hancock?" the doctor queried.

"Sir," Tyler said, nodding to the doctor.

As the doctor started to speak, Tyler couldn't do anything but watch his lips move. *This is not happening,* her mind screamed, *I can't lose her. Fuck.*

"I'm sorry, sir," Tyler said, holding up her hand. "Can you repeat that?"

"I said that Airman Devereaux lost a lot of blood, but she is resting comfortably. Fortunately, the bullet was a 22 caliber, so it didn't do too much damage. With some rest and rehabilitation, she'll be just fine."

"Thank you, sir," Tyler managed. The doctor nodded then walked away. Tyler found herself needing to lean against the nearest wall to catch her breath as the relief flooded her veins. *She's fine, she's fine,* she kept repeating to herself. "Damnit," she muttered to herself as she realized she'd forgotten to ask when she could see Shenin.

Walking over to the nurses' station, she quickly surveyed the women seated there. Smiling warmly at the younger woman sitting at the desk, she said, reading the girl's name tag, "Hi, Janet, I was wondering if you could tell me when I can see the airman from my team that was brought in wounded."

When Janet looked up, into Tyler's bright blue eyes, Tyler immediately recognized another gay soldier. Janet smiled, holding the eye contact for a moment longer than necessary, then she looked at her screen.

"Of course," she said, tapping the keys on the keyboard, "what's the airman's name?"

"Shenin Devereaux," Tyler replied.

Janet nodded, typing the name into the computer. "It looks like Airman Devereaux is still in recovery, so it's going to be a couple of hours before you can see her."

Tyler nodded, trying to decide how much she wanted to push it, but her need to see Shenin in person to know that she was really okay, overrode her usual caution about fraternizing while in uniform.

"I understand," she said, leaning on the counter between them, her smile displaying the dimples that tended to make women a little more amenable to anything she'd suggest. "Is that a full two hours," she asked, turning up the charm a little more. "Or are we talking about an hour and forty-five minutes? Maybe an hour and a half..." she said, letting her voice trail off hopefully. As she leaned forward putting more of her weight on the counter she was quickly reminded that the bullet wound in her forearm was still present, wincing as a pain shot through her arm.

"Oh, you're hurt too," Janet said, standing up and taking Tyler's arm gently.

"I'm fine," Tyler said, "it's just a scratch."

"Yeah, a scratch made by a 22 caliber bullet," came Sheila's voice from behind her. "How's Dev?" she asked Tyler, winking at Janet as she did.

"The doctor said she's okay," Tyler said, catching Sheila's look, "though Janet here was just telling me that we can't see her for another couple of hours."

Sheila considered the situation for a moment, then looked at Janet. "We really have to wait that long?" she asked. "You know, she was shot by a citizen that was a victim of the floods, right? Hell, she and Tyler here were being heroes, trying to protect that man's property, and he shot them, can you imagine?"

Janet looked between the two women. "Uh, no, I didn't realize that," she said, her look at Tyler chiding. "You didn't tell me you were a hero," she said, her smile bright.

"Well, that's Ty," Sheila said, waving dismissively, "she's not one to brag."

Tyler hid her grin behind her hand, knowing what Sheila was doing, and loving the girl for it.

"Well, I suppose it would be okay, if you just slipped in to see Airman Devereaux for a minute..." Janet said.

"That would be really great, Janet," Tyler said, seizing on the woman's momentary weakness. "I'd really appreciate it."

"She'd probably even take you to dinner to show her appreciation," Sheila added, slyly.

Tyler glanced at Sheila, thinking that now she wanted to smack the girl. *Thanks for the set-up, Sheila!*

"Oh, that wouldn't be necessary," Janet said, her tone completely unconvincing, even as a hopeful look lit her eyes.

"Of course it is," Sheila said, giving Tyler a look from behind Janet.

Tyler caught the look, narrowing her eyes slightly at Sheila, even as she smiled warmly at Janet. "Airman Welch is right, Janet, I know you'd be taking a chance letting me go back, so it's absolutely necessary for me to thank you properly." The intense smile was back, and Janet did everything but swoon at seeing it.

A couple of minutes later, Tyler was walking into the recovery room. Machines beside the bed were beeping; it was the only sound in the quiet room. An IV hung on a pole beside the bed, dripping constantly. Looking down at her best friend, Tyler could see that Shenin's shoulder was bandaged, and there was a bruise on her cheek, likely where she'd struck the side of the Humvee when the bullet had hit her. Tyler had to immediately tamp down on the sick feeling that picture conjured up in her head; she closed her eyes for a minute waiting for it to pass. When she opened her eyes, she saw Shenin's gold colored eyes staring back at her.

"You okay?" Shenin asked, her voice weak, her look concerned.

"Who's lying in a hospital bed here," Tyler asked, grinning, "me or you?"

"Good point," Shenin said, blinking slowly. It was obvious she was still groggy from the anesthesia.

Tyler moved to sit in the chair next to the bed, her eyes scanning Shenin's face as if checking every inch of it visually would ensure that her friend was okay. She grimaced as her eyes came back to the bruise on Shenin's face.

"Shen..." she said, reaching out to touch the bruise gently.

It's what they talked about in books and movies, almost as if she'd just touched a live wire, the jolt went through her. *You fucking idiot,* her head screamed at her, *you just fell in love with your best friend! Your STRAIGHT best friend!!* It was something she'd suspected for a while now, but she hadn't wanted to face it, or deal with it, and she definitely didn't want to do that now. So she shoved it down and did her best to keep the realization off her face. But it was too late, Shenin had caught the sudden look of sheer self-exasperation on Tyler's face before she managed to hide it.

"What?" Shenin asked, not one to ignore a look like that, but having literally no idea what the look was about.

"What?" Tyler replied, pretending that Shenin had imagined it would work in her weakened state.

No such luck.

"What was that look, Ty?" Shenin asked, her voice growing stronger again.

"There was no look, Dev," Tyler said, purposely using the nickname the unit had for Shenin, rather than the nickname Tyler usually used for her.

Shenin narrowed her eyes at the use of the alternate nickname, but decided she was fighting a losing battle with no real energy to fight it at this point, so she let it go. She knew that when Tyler didn't want to tell her something, there was usually a good reason. Normally she wanted to know what that good reason was, but tonight she didn't have the energy to drag it out of her friend. Rather than admit defeat, Shenin simply closed her eyes again, letting herself slip back into slumber.

Tyler watched her friend go back to sleep, her lips twitching in agitation. She didn't feel good about shutting Shenin down like that, but she also knew she was nowhere near ready to tell Shenin what was happening in her head. She wasn't sure she'd ever want to tell Shenin the truth.

A week after being shot, Shenin began physical therapy to ensure that her shoulder muscles would continue to do what she needed them to, in order to do her job. The session was grueling, but Shenin was determined. She'd been amazed by the support she'd received from her unit. There were six women on the team: Sheila, Jean, Tyler, Tina, Camilla and her. All five of the other women were encouraging her to get back into action. She'd even been given a commendation from the

Air Force, for her actions in the field. Sheila, Jean and Tyler had received one as well. The owner of the home had received probation and an order to get into rehabilitation for his drinking problem. As it turned out, there had been trouble at the house earlier in the day, and the men had threatened to return. The owner of the house had thought the Air Force squadron was that man and his friends. The homeowner had come to the hospital and apologized to Shenin profusely. She'd known it would be impossible for her to press charges against a man who'd just lost almost everything he owned in the floods.

Shenin had noted that Tyler hadn't been around much during the last week. Tyler claimed that she was working extra shifts to continue to help with the flood clean up. Shenin was fairly certain she was volunteering so she could avoid seeing her. Another development from her temporary fame, was that a member of the Thunderbirds, the Air Force's aerial demonstration squad, had asked her out. He was an almost impossibly handsome pilot in a squad of incredibly impressive pilots. It was definitely an interesting proposition, one Shenin hadn't been foolish enough to say no to.

Shenin was lying on her bunk dressed in her Air Force sweat pants and tank top when Tyler came in later in the evening, one arm thrown up over her eyes. Tyler felt an instant twinge of guilt, when she remembered that Shenin had been to her first physical therapy session that day. Tyler knew she'd been avoiding Shenin and that it wasn't fair. It was through no fault of Shenin's that Tyler was now terrified that Shenin would figure out that she was crushing on her.

"Hey," Tyler said. "How'd it go?"

Shenin lifted her arm off one eye. "Exhausting."

Tyler nodded. "Are you really sore?"

Shenin moved to sit up, rolling her shoulder as she did, and wincing. "You could say that," she said, grinning.

Tyler walked over to sit next to her on the bunk, taking Shenin's shoulders and turning her so that Shenin's bad shoulder was closer to her. Tyler proceeded to gently massage Shenin's injured shoulder, carefully avoiding the surgical incision, but working to smooth the bunched muscles around the spot. Slowly, but surely Shenin could feel her muscles start to ease. She closed her eyes and the warmth of Tyler's hands soothed the soreness away.

"Oh my god, you are good at this..." Shenin said, her tone trance-like.

Tyler grinned. "That's what I've heard," she said, her tone light.

"So what's on your agenda tonight?" Shenin asked, her eyes still closed, as Tyler continued to rub her shoulder.

"Got a date," Tyler said, "with a nurse from the Air Force hospital."

"Oh," Shenin said, grinning now. "I'm in ICU and you're making dates."

Tyler laughed. "Actually, I ended up having to take her out, so I could come back and see you in recovery."

"So it's my fault," Shenin surmised.

"Technically, it is," Tyler said, smiling.

"Uh-huh," Shenin said, her tone sarcastic, "I'm sure it's gonna break your heart to take this girl out."

"Not really, she's pretty cute," Tyler said.

"Then I'd say, you can *thank* me now," Shenin said.

"Yeah, you got shot so I could get a date?"

"That's just how good of a friend I am," Shenin said, breezily.

"Yeah, uh-huh," Tyler said, laughing now. Shenin laughed too. "So, what's on your agenda for tonight?" Tyler asked.

"Shower, Motrin and sleep," Shenin said. "In that order."

"Big night," Tyler said.

"Yeah, I'm a party animal."

"Party hamster, is more like it," Tyler corrected.

Shenin laughed.

"Is this better?" Tyler asked, gently squeezing her shoulder.

"Yes, thank you," Shenin said, nodding. "Now a hot shower should finish the job. But you go first, since you have a date."

"Okay," Tyler said, moving to get up.

Three hours later, Shenin was showered, medicated and happily sleeping when the thunderstorm started. She woke with a start at the first huge crack of thunder. Pulling her pillow over her head, she made the mistake of bringing up her injured arm to cover her head, letting out a yelp of pain, and felt tears sting her eyes immediately.

Across town, Tyler was having dinner with Janet, when the first flash of lightning caught her eye. She winced, knowing that Shenin was alone; everyone else from the unit was either on duty or out for the night since it was a Friday. Not that anyone else in the unit knew about Shenin's phobia about thunderstorms, but she would at least be able to talk to someone to distract herself if there were others around. Tyler knew there was no hope of saving this date. She made her apologies to Janet and headed back to the barracks as fast as she could.

As she expected, Shenin was buried under her pillow and shuddered every time thunder fired off. Taking off her jacket and kicking off her boots, Tyler knelt down next to Shenin's bunk, touching her on the arm. Shenin jumped, but pulled the pillow up to see Tyler kneeling there.

"What happened to your date?" she asked.

"Something came up," Tyler answered honestly.

Shenin narrowed her eyes at Tyler. "Like your chicken shit roommate being afraid of thunderstorms?" she asked.

"Maybe," Tyler said, moving to lie down next to the smaller girl and taking her gently in her arms.

"It's not your job to save me all the time, you know," Shenin said, as she snuggled against Tyler, welcoming the distraction from the storm, and the security that Tyler's arms always seemed to provide.

"I know," Tyler said, glancing down, and shivering slightly as, once again, Shenin's hand clasped the shirt at her waist. "But you don't have your date with the manly Thunderbird till next week," she said, hoping that her tone didn't sound as jealous as she felt.

Shenin didn't say anything, she thought she heard jealousy in Tyler's tone, but wasn't willing to ask her about it. She was enjoying feeling close to her friend again, and didn't want to spoil it. Her wonderfully gallant friend had left a date with a hot nurse, to be there for her so she wasn't going to complain.

"Technically, can you go out with him?" Tyler asked, grinning. "With the *thunder* and all?"

"You mean, in the squad name?" Shenin laughed.

"Yeah," Tyler grinned.

"I think I'll worry more about the fraternization thing."

"Ah, yeah, that's probably smart," Tyler agreed. "So, that brings up another question," Tyler then said.

"What's that?" Shenin asked.

"What if you two hit it off?"

"It's not like that's never happened," Shenin pointed out.

"Yeah, and one of them had to leave the military," Tyler said. "I doubt you're done with your career just yet, are you?"

"Tyler, it's one date!" Shenin said. "Not true love, sheesh."

Tyler shrugged. "Still against regs," she said, knowing she was being petty, and that it had nothing to do with the idea that officers and enlisted weren't allowed to fraternize.

"Well, it won't be soon," Shenin shot back, feeling defensive.

"What does that mean?" Tyler asked.

Shenin pressed her lips together, she hadn't meant to tell Tyler this way, but it was too late now.

"I got accepted to OTS," Shenin said.

"You what?" Tyler responded, floored. Shenin was telling her that she'd been accepted to Officer Training School. It meant she could get stationed somewhere else, once she received her commission.

"I finished my bachelor's degree at Beale, and had applied for OTS right before I came here. It took a while for my application and stuff to follow me."

Tyler stared back at her, shocked. "And when do you report?"

"Well, this injury put it off, but I have less than three months till I go."

Tyler blinked, trying to tamp down on the feeling of betrayal that slid through her.

"So, you already did your AFOQT and everything?" Tyler asked. Shenin nodded. "Your MEPS?"

"Yes, Tyler, yes, I've already been accepted by the selection board too. I'm going to be an officer."

Tyler nodded, accepting what she was being told. Part of her wondered if somehow this had happened for a reason, and that it was better this way. It was the way she had to accept what was happening.

They were both silent for a while as the storm raged outside.

"I'm sorry, Ty," Shenin said, finally. "This isn't how I wanted to tell you."

Tyler sighed. "It's okay," she said. "I guess I was just busy being a bitch."

"You weren't being a bitch, Ty, you were trying to warn me."

"You sure about that?" Tyler asked, being honest for a moment.

Shenin looked up at her in the semi darkness of the room, trying to gauge her friend's mood. Instead of answering, she reached up and laid her hand on Tyler's cheek. She then laid her head against Tyler's shoulder again. It was her way of forgiving her but also helping them move on. Once again, Tyler found herself grateful for Shenin's way of handling things at times. They were both quiet for a while, Shenin shaking slightly every time the thunder cracked, Tyler gently hugging her close when she did.

"So, how cute is she?" Shenin asked.

"Who?" Tyler asked, her mind having been miles away, thinking about how much she'd miss this kind of thing when Shenin was an officer and probably stationed somewhere else.

"The nurse from the hospital," Shenin said.

"Oh," Tyler said, grinning, "yeah, she's pretty cute."

"Gonna reschedule your date with her?"

Tyler looked down at her, her look measured, was she imagining the slight tinge of concern there? Of course she was, what was she thinking?

"Probably," she said, shrugging. "It's been awhile."

Shenin's eyes widened. "Do you do that?"

"Do what?" Tyler asked.

"You know, go out with women just to get…"

"Laid?" Tyler supplied.

"Yeah," Shenin said.

Tyler thought about it for a minute. "Not a lot, no," she said honestly, "but, sometimes that's what it is. "

"And this nurse would be okay with that?"

"Uhhh… Well, that's not like the first question I ask, usually," Tyler said, grinning at the way Shenin was looking at her. "What?"

"You're a tramp!" Shenin said, laughing.

"I have my moments…" Tyler said.

"Uh-huh," Shenin said, nodding, "and how does that go?"

"Like how do I get a girl to sleep with me?" Tyler asked, highly amused that Shenin was asking all of this.

"Yeah," Shenin said, curious in spite of herself.

Tyler looked back at her for a long moment, but decided it wouldn't hurt to try and answer her friend's question.

"Well, it isn't like I have a specific line or anything," she said. "But most women want the same thing."

"And what's that?"

"Women want to be heard, they want to know that someone is interested in what they think, what they feel, what they want."

Shenin considered that answer, and had to agree with her friend.

"And they usually want you, don't they?" she heard herself asking.

Tyler narrowed her eyes slightly. "Not always," she said, "but you need to know that I'm not only ever looking to score."

"No, you wouldn't be," Shenin said, her tone confident.

Tyler grinned, canting her head. "What does that mean?"

"It means, that someone like you wouldn't only ever be trying to get into a woman's pants," Shenin said, her eyes staring up at Tyler in the semi-darkness.

"Okay... where is this coming from?" Tyler asked, trying to follow Shenin's logic.

"You're way too gallant to be like that," Shenin replied.

"Gallant?" Tyler repeated, finding the term odd.

"Yeah, that's what you are, Ty, you're gallant."

"Uhhh," Tyler stammered, "okay?"

Shenin sighed. "Look at this, right here," she said, gesturing between them. "You're here because you know I'm afraid of a thunderstorm, who does stuff like that?"

"Uhh..." Tyler stammered again, not sure what to say in this instance.

"Not many people, Tyler, but you do. You carry my bags, you open doors for me, you run into gunfire to keep me safe."

Tyler looked shocked at that last statement.

"Didn't know I knew that, did you?" Shenin asked, knowing the answer.

"Uh, well, no, not really… no," Tyler said.

"Yeah, I figured as much," Shenin said. "You have no idea what an awesome person you are, Tyler, do you? Any woman would be lucky to have you in her life. So, I'd say if the nurse is smart, she'll sleep with you, if you want her to."

Tyler laughed out loud at that statement. "Really now?"

"Yep," Shenin replied, "sure as shit."

"Sure as shit?" Tyler replied, chuckling.

"Yep," Shenin replied.

"I see," Tyler said, shaking her head.

"What do you see?"

"That you're nuts," Tyler replied, laughing again.

"Maybe, but you watch, I'm right."

CHAPTER 3

Two weeks later, Tyler found out that Shenin was indeed right. Not only did Janet sleep with her, but she also wouldn't stop calling her.

"Good God, is that her again?" Sheila asked, as Tyler checked her phone for the fifth time during their shift.

"Yeah," Tyler said, sending the call to voicemail again.

"How good *are* you in bed?" Sheila said, rolling her eyes. "Maybe I should sleep with you."

"Is that an offer?" Tyler asked, grinning.

"Maybe," Sheila replied, laughing.

"Right, and I'm a general."

"That would just get you more tail," Sheila pointed out.

Tyler laughed.

"I heard about Dev going to OTS," Sheila said then. "That sucks."

"Yeah, it does, but it's good for her, I think she'd make a good officer."

"She will, you're right," Sheila said. "But she'll be a major loss to the team."

"True," Tyler said, her look far away suddenly.

Sheila narrowed her eyes at her friend. "What's going on there?" she asked.

"What?" Tyler replied, her tone completely normal.

Sheila looked back at her friend for a moment, and thought that maybe she'd just imagined what she thought she'd seen.

"Nothing," Sheila said, shrugging. "When does she leave?"

"In September," Tyler replied, relieved that she'd played off Sheila's suspicions; her life would be hell if Sheila knew that she had a major thing for Shenin. Sheila already had the tendency to meddle so the last thing Tyler wanted was for Sheila to tell Shenin about her feelings for her. She was bound and determined to get through this, and out of this, with at least a shred of dignity. As it was, it took everything she had half of the time not to beg Shenin not to go. It was better for everyone if Shenin went away; it was going to be nothing but a disaster for everyone, especially Tyler, if she stayed.

"We need to have a party," Sheila said.

"Yeah, we do," Tyler agreed.

Shenin had been on two dates with Dan. She'd enjoyed the first date; he was personable, if a bit egotistical. She attributed his ego to the fact that he was a great pilot, and tried to ignore the annoying nagging feeling that he was just trying to get some. He'd been a perfect gentleman the first night, though, and when he'd dropped her off at her car, he'd kissed her on the cheek. They'd driven separately to a location, so that they would not be observed going out together. Their second date had ended much the same, but this time he'd kissed her on the lips. They were now on their third date, and this time he'd suggested that they go back to his apartment off base for "a night cap", which she took as code for more than a chaste kiss on the lips. She figured it had been a long time for her in the sex department; it might just be time to get some herself. So she'd agreed to go to his apartment.

Two hours later she was wishing heartily that she'd said no. She lay in her bunk, trying to think of anything but the scene at his apartment. The anger, shame and humiliation burned through her, and hurt at least as much as her shoulder at this point. She couldn't believe what had happened.

He'd been all charm and sweetness. When he'd leaned in to kiss her on the couch in his expensive apartment, she'd told herself she was ready for this. As their lips met, she found that he was a decent kisser, maybe a little lackluster, and not quite what she'd expected, but she ignored that. Within minutes though, his hands were all over her, and pulling at her clothes as he pushed her back on the couch. Suddenly an alarm had gone off in her head, and it had her pushing at him to get him off her. He'd backed off temporarily, but within a few minutes, he was pushing himself up on her again, this time more aggressively. This time when she'd tried to push him off, he'd tightened his hand on her throat, and had her using every ounce of strength she could muster to shove him. He'd landed hard against the coffee table, and she could see he was instantly infuriated, so she leaped to her feet, staving him off.

"I know your career isn't worth a piece of ass," she told him, her tone all security force, her eyes blazing. "Touch me again, and I'll make sure you go down in flames."

That had him hesitating. She knew she had him there, and that he wasn't going to be stupid enough to push this any farther. It made her wonder how many other women had been willing to let him force himself on them. She'd beat a hasty retreat, calling a taxi from her cell phone outside his apartment building. Her shoulder was aching wildly at that point, and her throat burned a bit from where he'd grabbed her. She wasn't really ready to closely examine what just happened, she just put herself on auto pilot and got herself to her car, and back to the barracks.

Tyler walked into their room about an hour after Shenin had gotten in. She noted that Shenin was curled into a ball on her bunk, and instantly went on high alert, it wasn't the way her friend usually slept, so something was wrong.

"Shen?" Tyler whispered, as she sat down on the side of Shenin's bunk.

Shenin didn't lift her head. "Hmm?" she asked, feigning sleep.

"You okay?" Tyler asked.

"Mmmhmm," Shenin replied, not wanting to outright lie.

Tyler narrowed her eyes at that, she noted that Shenin didn't say "yes." Reaching down, she stroked Shenin's hair, trying to sense what was really happening with her friend. That's when she heard the sniffle. Brushing Shenin's hair aside, she touched her cheek feeling moisture.

“Why are you crying?” Tyler asked, her tone suspicious.

Shenin didn’t answer for a moment.

“And don’t try lying to me,” Tyler said, “I know you too well for that.”

Shenin peaked up at Tyler with one eye, trying to figure out what she could say to diffuse this whole thing. She knew what getting Tyler involved in this matter would do.

“It was just a bad night,” she said then, hoping Tyler would take that and let her be. No such luck.

“Uh-huh,” Tyler muttered, “and?”

Shenin wasn’t a crier, so something pretty big must have happened to cause her to lie in the dark and cry.

“Ty, I just want to go to sleep, okay?”

Tyler considered her options. She could push it with Shenin, and likely upset her more, or she could leave it alone, and hope that she’d talk about it when she was ready. She opted for the latter.

“Okay,” she said, gently brushing away a tear with her thumb, making Shenin have to literally hold her breath to keep from sobbing out loud. “I’m here if you want to talk.”

All Shenin could do was to nod, not wanting to take the chance that her voice would choke up on her if she tried to speak. She just wanted this night to be over.

When she woke in the morning, she glanced at her bedside clock and realized Tyler wouldn’t be up for another half hour. She decided to take a nice long, hot shower, to try and soak out some of the soreness. She was just getting out of the shower and wrapping a towel around her when she heard Tyler's voice.

"Hey don't use all the hot water," Tyler was saying as she walked in, but then stopped dead in her tracks. "What the fuck?" she practically yelled.

Shenin looked up to see that Tyler was looking at her, at her neck... *oh shit* was all she had time to think before Tyler strode over, taking her chin in her thumb and forefinger and tilting her chin up.

"What the fuck happened?" Tyler asked, already sure she knew.

"Ty..." Shenin began trying to back up. Tyler's hand at the back of her neck stopped her instantly.

"Don't fucking try to tell me nothing happened, Shenin, I won't believe that. Did he do this?" There was murder in those very blue eyes, and Shenin actually feared for Dan's life at that moment.

"Yes, but..."

"He's fucking dead!" Tyler said, letting Shenin go, and turning on her heel to stride out of the bathroom.

"Tyler!" Shenin screamed, running after her, catching up to her at her bunk, she was pulling on her boots. "You can't!"

"Like hell I can't," Tyler said, tying her boots with sharp movements. "He's a dead man, Shenin, that's all there is to this."

"He's an officer!" Shenin shouted.

"Like I fucking care!" Tyler yelled back, standing up to reach for her shirt.

"Ty, listen to me!" Shenin said, reaching up to stop Tyler's movement, there were tears in her eyes now.

Tyler looked down at the other girl, and saw the tears, instantly losing some of her steam. "Please don't do that," she said, her voice softening.

"You have to listen to me, Ty, you have to," Shenin said, reaching up to touch Tyler's cheek. "He's an asshole, yes, he deserves to be castrated, yes, but he's an officer, and I'm not, and if I report this, I'll never be one."

Tyler took a deep breath as she considered what Shenin was saying. Shenin was right, if she reported Dan's attack on her, she'd ruin his career, but she'd ruin hers too. Closing her eyes slowly, Tyler forced herself to calm down. Opening her eyes, she looked down at Shenin again, her eyes searching her friend's eyes.

"I could kill him quietly, no one would need to know..." she said, grinning.

Shenin smiled through her tears. With that Tyler lost it, and had to pull her into her arms, tears stinging the backs of her eyelids as she closed her eyes, holding Shenin to her. "I'm so sorry this happened to you," she whispered against Shenin's ear.

That was when Shenin lost all of her composure, bursting into tears. This was how men should be; this was how they should act. This is what women want, they want to be heard, and loved, and treated like they are made of glass. Tyler tightened her hold on the other girl, holding her close and stroking her hair. When Shenin continued to cry, Tyler moved to sit on her bunk, pulling Shenin down on her lap and cradled her. Shenin buried her face in Tyler's hair that was still loose, as she hadn't put it up for the day yet.

"Go ahead," Tyler said, grinning. "I have to wash it anyway."

Shenin laughed in spite of her tears. Tyler couldn't help but smile.

"Why can't you be a man?" Shenin asked, thinking along the lines she had when she'd lost her composure.

"Because I have a uterus?" Tyler replied, making Shenin laugh again.

"Good point," Shenin said.

It took a few more minutes, but finally Shenin calmed. She was also able to hide the bruises Dan's fingers had left on her throat with cover-up and make-up. Dan received a very distinct message from a member of the security force that day. Tyler strode up to him on the flight line, her blue eyes staring straight into his as she first saluted him, and awaited his return salute. Then she leaned in looking up at him intensely and simply stated, "If you ever touch her again, I'll kill you, officer or not." With that, she took one step back, pivoted to her right, and strode away.

Dan watched her go, and didn't doubt for a minute that she'd carry out her threat, he'd been able to see it in her eyes. He may be a pilot, but he knew a serious threat when he saw it, and he also knew that a member of the security force wasn't someone you wanted to make an enemy of.

Shenin spent a lot of time working through her shoulder pain, she knew she needed to be fully prepared for the physical aspect of the Officer Training School. She had to almost physically push aside some of the thoughts that kept crowding in while she lifted weights and ran miles and miles. Her thoughts kept coming back to Tyler, and how deeply attached to her, she was. She wasn't foolish enough to think that the attachment she felt for Tyler was simple friendship, or gratitude, it was more, she just wasn't sure how much more.

CHAPTER 4

The time flew by, and before long it was the night before Shenin was scheduled to leave for OTS in Alabama. Sheila and Tyler had arranged a party for her that included the members of the team, all of whom were fully aware of the sexual orientation of their teammates. It also included other friends that wanted to help celebrate the occasion.

Sandra's home was considered a safe zone, and only people who could be completely trusted were ever invited there. Sandra was an old friend; she had served alongside Tyler and Sheila for a while, before Shenin had joined the team. Since leaving the military, her home had turned into somewhat of a refuge for gay military personnel, away from the confines of Don't Ask, Don't Tell… and it was also a great spot for a party!

There was a lot of drinking, laughing, storytelling and music. One rousing rendition of Pink's 'Raise Your Glass', especially the line, "So raise your glass if you are wrong, in all the right ways, all the underdogs, we will never be anything but loud, dirty little freaks," had everyone singing at the top of their lungs.

"So, where is your family?" Jean asked Shenin at one point. They were all sitting around the patio table, the music playing in the background. Most of them were drinking beer; Shenin was drinking a margarita as were a couple of others. It was hot in Vegas, so many people were sitting around in bikini tops and shorts. Shenin wore a Hawaiian print bikini top and fairly short black bike shorts. Whereas Tyler was wearing an Air Force tank top, and dark blue board shorts. It was a graphic illustration in the difference between them. Shenin was every bit the girly girl and though Tyler was not what would be considered butch in the lesbian community, she was definitely a "soft butch". Shenin had always admired Tyler's style, she didn't wear make-up, but kept her curly hair long. She dressed to fit her body style, but was never flashy.

"California," Shenin said, answering Sheila's question, "Sacramento."

"And you were stationed at Beale?"

"Yep," Shenin said, smiling. "I know, it was pure luck that first time out."

"Yeah, it never seems to happen that way," Tyler said. "I've asked for Andrews so many times, I'm almost thinking if I don't ask for it, they'll give it to me."

Everyone laughed, nodding. It seemed to be a trend that the last place you listed as an option was always the place you ended up in.

"Your family is in D.C., isn't it?" Sheila asked.

"No, southern Maryland, but it's the closest base to home, yeah," Tyler answered.

"She's related to half of Maryland," Shenin put in.

"That's right, you went home with her last time, didn't you?" Sheila asked.

Shenin nodded.

"How'd that go?" Sheila asked, remembering the conversation she'd had with Tyler about how her parents had taken her coming out. She knew it had been devastating for Tyler, and that the last trip home had been the first in five years.

Tyler nodded. "It went okay," she said. "Most of my family was totally cool with the gay thing."

Shenin shook her head, looking surprised. "I just can't fathom that," she said to no one in particular.

"Fathom what?" Tyler asked.

Shenin looked over at her, her eyes softening slightly. "Having to handle your family not accepting who you are."

"It happens a lot in our community," Teri put in.

"I know," Shenin said, her tone empathetic, "it's terrible." When everyone just looked at her, she went on, "Why should someone's sexual preference matter? Your parents are supposed to love you, no matter what. That's part of being a parent, knowing that your kids are going to make their own choices in life, and that you have to love them no matter what those choices are."

"So, you subscribe to the idea that being gay is a choice?" Sheila asked, raising an eyebrow at the younger girl.

Shenin considered the question for a moment. "I think sometimes it's a choice."

"Really?" Tyler asked, surprised by Shenin's answer, "why do you think that?"

Shenin looked back at her friend for a long moment. "I know for you it wasn't a choice, it was something you discovered about yourself. I'm sure it would have made your life so much easier had you not been gay. I'm sure it would have been easier for a lot of you, and a lot of people if they hadn't been born gay, but that's not something you can control. But I do think that other people will decide to be gay."

"In this world, why would anyone choose that?" Jean asked.

"Well," Shenin said, her eyes on Tyler again, "if you put a woman in the right situation with another woman, and you put enough men in that woman's past, that have abused her, or hurt her. I think that any woman can decide to be with another woman, instead of a man."

"What kind of situation are we talking about?" Sheila asked, curious now.

Shenin shrugged. "I don't know, maybe a woman has been dating men, and they've been terrible examples of men, abusive, mean, or just plain useless."

"Which is most of them," Jean put in, grinning.

"I second that," Tyler said, raising her hand and grinning too.

"Me too," came from a few of the other women in the group.

"Then you put that same woman with someone like…" she said, looking right at Tyler, "like Tyler, or one of you ladies, and she's bound to realize that a woman is likely to treat her better than the men in her life have."

"Sounds like someone may be earning a toaster soon," Sheila said, her grin wry, as she nodded toward Tyler.

"Fuck you," Tyler said, narrowing her eyes, but grinning all the while.

"You wish," Sheila shot back, grinning too.

"Girls, girls, you're both pretty," Jean said, using one of Tyler's favorite phrases to diffuse debates. Everyone laughed.

Shenin laughed too, but her eyes never left Tyler's.

Later, as the party was winding down, Shenin dragged Tyler onto the dance floor with her; they were dancing a slow dance to Billie Myer's 'Kiss the Rain'.

"So that was an interesting point of view," Tyler said, looking down at her friend.

Shenin looked up into Tyler's blue eyes, smiling. "It was honest," she said, simply.

"It made a lot of people think," Tyler said.

"Is that a bad thing?" Shenin asked.

"Never," Tyler replied, smiling.

Shenin stepped in closer, winding her arm tighter around Tyler's waist, and resting her head on her friend's shoulder. Tyler smiled fondly, wanting to hold onto this feeling, because she knew everything was going to change when Shenin left the next day. She had no idea if she'd ever see Shenin again, and it was breaking her heart, she was doing her best to hide it, but she wasn't sure if she was succeeding at all.

The lyrics of the song that played seemed to be playing out her worst fear. The song talked about the distance between two people that could develop when they were apart, and that things like phone calls wouldn't bridge that distance. Tyler was afraid that it was what their friendship would be reduced to: phone calls or emails that were one sided, and that would taper off, and eventually stop altogether. Tyler hadn't been in this situation before; she wasn't sure what to do about it. And in truth there was nothing she could or would do about it. Shenin was straight, she was also career Air Force, and there was no way Tyler would ever endanger that by pushing for something that would probably never be what she really wanted anyway. It just wasn't something that was in the cards, it just sucked.

"Ty?" Shenin said, interrupting the direction of her thoughts.

"Hmmm?" Tyler murmured trying her best to pull herself out of the dark mood she was quickly slipping into.

"Can we go somewhere else and talk?" Shenin asked.

Tyler looked down at her for a long moment, trying to decide if this would be a good idea, considering the direction of her thoughts that moment.

"Ty?" Shenin repeated, not sure what the look in Tyler's eyes meant, but wanting to get away from the group for a few minutes.

"Huh, oh, yeah, of course," Tyler said, shaking her head to clear it. Taking Shenin's hand, she led her to one of the bedrooms on the second floor of the house. Checking the room to ensure it was clear she led Shenin in and closed the door behind them.

"What's up, Shen?" Tyler asked, feeling very jumpy all of a sudden.

"Can we sit down?" Shenin asked, gesturing to the bed.

"Uh..." Tyler stammered, thinking that was probably not a good idea. It hit her then that she'd had a lot to drink, and maybe her judgment wasn't exactly sound at that moment.

"Jesus, Hancock, I'm not going to attack you," Shenin said, her tone sharper than she'd meant. Tyler had been far away all night, and it was really starting to worry Shenin.

"I know that," Tyler snapped, in response to Shenin's tone, but then blew her breath out. The last thing she wanted was to have a big wicked fight with her best friend the night before she was leaving. "I'm sorry," she said, her tone sincere. "Please," she said, then gesturing for Shenin to precede her. Shenin grinned as she moved to sit down.

"What?" Tyler asked, seeing the grin.

"Always the gentleman," Shenin murmured.

"Stop it," Tyler replied, but grinned.

When they were both seated on the bed, facing each other, Shenin took Tyler's hands in hers, noticing how cold they were. She automatically started rubbing them to try to warm them; even as she began the speech she'd had rolling around in her head for weeks now.

"Tyler Hancock, you are, without a doubt the very best friend I've ever had, you know that right?"

"Shen," Tyler began, her tone forestalling, "you don't have to do this…"

"Tyler," Shenin said, her tone strong, "shut up."

"Okay," Tyler said, snapping her mouth shut, as if she'd just been given an order by the highest general. Shenin couldn't help but laugh at the action.

"You're not helping here," Shenin told her.

Tyler pressed her lips together comically and nodded, her blue eyes sparkling with humor.

Shenin sighed, not sure why she ever thought that she'd be able to get through this thing without interruption or comments from her friend. She knew Tyler, and it was never going to be that easy. Finally, she just looked directly into her friend's eyes, and asked the question she knew she needed to.

"Why don't you want a toaster?" she asked, her eyes belying the casual meaning in her words.

Tyler stared back at her for a full minute, her mouth hanging slightly open. "I'm sorry, what?" she asked finally.

"Why don't you want a toaster," Shenin repeated, "for me?"

Tyler gave her friend a sidelong look. "Exactly how much have you had to drink tonight?"

"Tyler!" Shenin shouted, laughing in spite of herself.

"Shenin!" Tyler replied. "You're kind of sounding like a crazy person right now."

Shenin leaned forward, placing her forehead against Tyler's shirt, and rolling it back and forth woefully. "I'm doing this all wrong," she said.

"What are you trying to do, Shen?" Tyler asked.

Shenin just sighed loudly. Tyler put a finger under Shenin's chin and tilted her face up to hers. "Just tell me," she said, feeling a slight panic.

Shenin blinked a couple of times, obviously trying to gather her thoughts. Finally she blew her breath out in a gush. "Why don't you want me?" she asked, her tone rushed, like getting it out fast would keep it from sounding bad.

Tyler's brow furrowed, she seriously couldn't be asking that question could she? Surely she'd heard her wrong.

"I'm sorry, what did you say?"

"Tyler…" Shenin said.

"It sounded like you asked me why I don't want you." Tyler said.

"That's what I said," Shenin confirmed.

Tyler nodded. "I have no idea how to answer that," she said after a long pause.

Shenin looked stricken, and then started to nod as she began to stand up. Tyler's hand on her arm stopped her.

"Shen, wait," Tyler said, not sure what she was doing, it was probably better if Shenin thought she didn't want her, it would be easier all the way around. What Tyler couldn't handle, however, was the look of utter devastation on her friend's face, she couldn't let that be. Reaching out she touched Shenin's cheek, her look softening, "I never said I don't want you, Shen," she said softly, "I just can't be with you."

Shenin took that in for a moment, looking happy then confused. "Why?" she asked.

Tyler gave her a stern look. "Well, let's start with the fact that you're not gay."

"So, I'm gay-curious," Shenin said, her tone so earnest Tyler had to smile.

"Bi-curious," Tyler corrected.

"Huh?" Shenin queried, clearly confused.

"You sleep with guys. That doesn't make you gay, it makes you straight. If you're curious about the gay lifestyle it makes you bi, as in bi-sexual, curious."

"Oh," Shenin said simply, looking contrite.

Tyler grinned. "Tell me what you're curious about."

"It's not that easy, and you know it," Shenin said, her tone frustrated.

"What do you want to know?" Tyler asked.

Shenin sighed, shaking her head again. "I want to know why I think about you all the time, why every little thing you do makes me smile. I want to know why I can't stop wondering what it would be like to be in a relationship with someone like you, what dating someone like you would be like..."

"Is that all?" Tyler asked, grinning.

"Stop it!" Shenin said, shoving Tyler away from her, but grinning at the same time, and laughing when Tyler fell back on the bed.

"Hey!" Tyler said, grinning. "No violence here, missy."

"I'll show you violence," Shenin threatened, narrowing her eyes at her friend. "I'll hog tie you and shove you back in the closet!"

Tyler started laughing, just because the picture that it presented was far too funny. Shenin joined her, laughing too. Throwing herself down on the bed, lying next to Tyler, both of them on their back, they both had a good laugh. When they'd calmed down, Shenin turned over on her side, facing Tyler.

"Ty?"

"Hmmm?"

"Seriously, would you ever date me?"

Tyler considered the question, then shook her head. "No," she said.

"Why?" Shenin asked, surprised by how much she needed to know the answer.

"Well, for one, you're straight," Tyler began.

"Yeah, yeah we covered that," Shenin said, waving dismissively, which caused Tyler to grin again.

"For another thing, Shen, you're on your way to Officer Training School tomorrow. They're about to tell you about how evil being gay is, and how as an officer it's your job to ensure that the people under your command are completely moral and honest with the United States Air Force. It's going to be your job to find and get rid of people like me."

"I don't think they say evil," Shenin said, her tone petulant. "And you know how I feel about Don't Ask, Don't Tell."

"Subversive, bad for morale, you name it. It all comes down to the same thing. Gay is not okay in the military. And no matter how you feel about DADT it won't matter, as an officer you'll have to enforce it."

Shenin considered what Tyler was saying. "Obama's working on getting rid of Don't Ask, Don't Tell."

"Yeah, it's not going to happen, Shen, it's a gay pipe-dream."

Shenin swallowed convulsively. "So what if I didn't go to OTS tomorrow, what if I stayed enlisted and stay here."

"No," Tyler said, her tone stern.

"Tyler…" Shenin began.

"No, Shenin, I won't let you do that, not for me, not for anyone. This is what you want, if it wasn't, you wouldn't have applied. I'm never going to stand in your way, I won't do it. Besides, do you realize what this life is like? How hard it is? Constantly having to hide who you really are, afraid that you'll say the wrong thing, do the wrong thing, get seen by the wrong person, and then you're out. No pension, no benefits, no GI Bill, just a dishonorable discharge that will follow you forever, affect every aspect of your life. No," she said again, shaking her head, "I won't do that to you."

"But isn't it my choice?" Shenin asked.

"No, it's not," Tyler said her tone strong, "it's not your choice. It's my life too, it's my future too, and I can't have a future by ruining someone else's."

"But you do this, Tyler, you live this life," Shenin tried again, desperate to reason with her, astounded at how important this was becoming suddenly.

Tyler looked at her for a long moment, turning over on her side to face her. "Yeah," she said, "you're right, I live this life, and that's why I'm not going to condemn you to the same fate as me."

With that, Tyler got up off the bed and left the room. Shenin stayed on the bed, staring at the spot Tyler had been in moments before. The tears started then, she had no idea what to do now. She felt like her whole world was coming to an end. She thought she'd figured something out about herself, and she thought that Tyler was an answer to something. Now… now she had no idea what to think. She cried herself to sleep that night. Meanwhile, Tyler quietly got very drunk, finally leaving the house in the middle of the night to keep from going back to that room and doing what she'd wanted to do since the day she'd met Shenin Devereaux. Back in the barracks, thankfully in one piece, she passed out in her bunk. Early the next morning, she got up early and left the barracks, making sure she'd miss Shenin when she came to collect her gear to leave. It was the worst day of her life, and she spent it alone in a jeep at the far end of the flight line.

Chapter 5

Officer Training School was tough. Shenin found she didn't have a lot of time to think about anything but what she was there to do. There was a great deal of mental and physical aspects of the training. During the indoctrination phase, the officer candidates were tested on the confidence course, showing how they worked within a team; it involved grueling physical tests as well as learning how to be the leader of a team. The second phase involved things Shenin was more acclimated to: there was multicultural training, so officers understood how to adapt to different cultures. This second phase also included situational training, as well as ground combat skills and weapons training. Shenin was highly familiar with both hand-to-hand combat and with using weapons; she was easily able to attain her expert marksmanship badge during this phase. The third phase included the leadership challenge that taught the candidates about tactical movements.

In every phase the candidates were evaluated and given feedback. Shenin didn't remember being yelled at that much since basic training. It didn't faze her, however, since as a member of the security force, and a woman, guys were always getting in her face and yelling at them, she'd been trained to remain completely passive in appearance. The last phase involved the Air Expeditionary Force Exercise. It was more or less a final exam. By the end of the nine weeks, Shenin felt like she'd been put through the ringer more than once.

On graduation day, she was very happy to see her mother and her older brother in the stands. It had been a small hope that Tyler would somehow make it to the graduation, but Shenin knew she was being stupid. She hadn't heard a word from Tyler since that night at the party. She knew it was probably the way things were going to be from now on and that she needed to move on. She'd received orders to report to Eielson Air Force in Fairbanks, Alaska. It wasn't necessarily an optimal base, but she'd known going into OTS that she was unlikely to be assigned back to Nellis. She'd also learned that the average temperature in Fairbanks, Alaska in November was twelve degrees. It was certainly going to be different from Las Vegas.

After graduation, Shenin had ten days to report to Eielson. She went home to Sacramento, and did her best to not think about Tyler, where she was, what she was doing. The day before she was scheduled to leave for Fairbanks, Alaska, she got an email from Sheila. The email read:

Thought you should know that our unit has received orders for the Middle East, we're being deployed as of tomorrow. Hope OTS went well, knowing you, you graduated at the top of your class. Take good care. Shelia.

Shenin closed her eyes slowly after reading the email, all of her friends in the Middle East, all of them in danger, Tyler in danger. She felt sick. She had a moment's thought of resigning her commission and asking to go with her unit, but there was no guarantee she'd be allowed to go with them, and she also knew that Tyler would be infuriated at her for doing something so "dumb".

Instead she emailed Sheila back. Her email read:

OTS was fun, NOT! Please take very good care over there, and please watch each other's backs. Wish I was going to be there with you all. I'm headed to Fairbanks, Alaska. Please, please keep in touch and let me know how things are going over there. Much love, Dev.

It was all she could do, and she knew it, but it didn't make it any easier to handle. She spent her last day home in a fog.

"What's happening with you?" Trish asked her daughter that evening as they sat on the porch of the house. It was a nice evening; the Delta Breeze had come back up, cooling off downtown Sacramento.

Shenin looked over at her mom, not sure what to tell her. Her mom had always been her champion, no matter what. Shenin always figured it was because she'd always had to play mom and dad to her and her brother.

She sighed, shaking her head, "I just found out my unit at Nellis has been deployed to the Middle East, they leave tomorrow."

Trish looked back at her daughter, sensing that there was more to this than just general concern for her old unit. "Tyler's going with them?" she asked.

Shenin nodded, looking a little grave.

"And that's really what's bothering you, is it?" Trish asked.

Shenin looked back at her mother for a long moment, which had Trish grinning.

"I'm not blind, Shenin Doaha," Trish said, her tone chiding. "I know you have very deep feelings for Tyler."

"Why do you say that?" Shenin asked, curious what she'd done to let that on to her mother.

"I've known you your whole life, babe," her mom said. "You've never had a lot of friends, always just one or two special ones, but even they didn't inspire the kind of loyalty that being friends with Tyler has for you. It doesn't take a rocket scientist to understand what's happening there."

"And what do you think is happening there?" Shenin asked.

Trish smiled fondly and said, "You're in love with her."

Shenin's mouth dropped open in shock, it took her a minute to find her voice, but then she had no idea what to say for another minute.

"Is that what you think?" she asked her mother.

Trish considered for a moment and then nodded. "That's what I would guess, yeah."

"And you got this from?" Shenin asked.

"From the way you talked about her when you called on the phone, it was Tyler did this, Tyler said that, from the way you described her mannerisms, the way she was with you. I figured she was in love with you, and it wouldn't take much to make that feeling mutual."

"You think she's in love with me?"

The look Trish gave her daughter was of utter disbelief. "You didn't know that?"

Shenin once again found her mouth open, then her brain reeled back to their last conversation, Tyler's words, "I live this life, and that's why I'm not going to condemn you to the same fate as me." And then her mind went to all the times Tyler had been there for her, even leaving a date to be with her during a thunderstorm. Then her thoughts turned to the night she'd been shot. Tyler had run toward the gunfire to get the guy that had shot her, and at the hospital, there had been a definite shift in Tyler's thoughts. And Tyler was far too gallant to, on the one hand tell her she was in love with her, and then on the other say they couldn't be together. She'd fall on her sword to keep Shenin at bay, and keep her out of the gay lifestyle.

"That little shit," Shenin muttered.

Trish started to laugh. "Just figured it out, huh?"

"Shut up, mom," Shenin said, grinning.

That night, lying in her childhood bed, Shenin's mind went over and over every moment with Tyler, and the more she thought about it, the more she realized she'd been completely blind to Tyler's feelings. The way she'd reacted the morning she'd seen the bruises on her throat that Dan had caused, Shenin had been sure Tyler was going to kill him with her bare hands. It had terrified her at the time because assaulting an officer would have had Tyler thrown in the stockade and out of the military faster than she could blink. But now it made sense; it made sense that Tyler had sounded jealous about her going out with Dan in the first place and bringing up the regulations, when she herself was breaking regulations all the time by not only being gay, but dating other service women. It all made sense and now it was too late. She did the only thing she could. She got out of bed, started her computer and sent Tyler an email:

I heard from Sheila that you guys are being deployed. I'm sorry about how things ended up with us before I left for OTS. You were looking out for me, because let's face it, that's what you've done for me since the day we met. Tyler, you need to know that are the most important person in the world to me. You need to take the very best care over there, because I need you to come back. Please be safe and please write me if you have the time. I can handle anything else, but I just need to know you're okay? My heart will be with you over there, I wish that I could be there to back you up. Love, Shen.

As she hit send on the email, she felt a little bit better. Maybe Tyler would ignore the email, maybe not, but at least she had sent it and felt like that was the most she could do at this point. She hoped with every fiber of her being that Tyler would answer.

Eielson Air Force Base was covered with snow when she arrived. Her first impression of the base was that it was a big chunk of ice. The young airman that picked her up chatted comfortably all the way to the base office.

"Oh yeah, we got the first really big snow a week ago, and they're predicting another big storm for the end of the week. Hope you brought your warm weather gear," he said, smiling over at the pretty new officer.

"Don't really have much," Shenin said. "I'm coming from Nellis."

"Oh, well, you'll need to get over to the supply officer right away. Nellis huh? How was that? I'd think it would be awesome to be stationed in Vegas."

"It's hot," Shenin said, grinning. "But it did have its moments."

"That's really cool," the young man said, his smile bright.

He was glad that this new lieutenant seemed really nice. Officers were hard to gauge sometimes. New officers tended to be full of themselves. Some of them were very strict about being saluted by enlisted personnel, or ordered people around, just because they could. This new lieutenant didn't seem to be that type at all.

Later in the security force office, Shenin got a chance to meet the captain she'd be working with. His name was Bill Chapman "Chappy," he was older, she figured he was probably in his fifties. When he walked into his outer office, Shenin stood up immediately, snapping to attention and saluting him. He looked down at her, his eyes taking in her youth, her uniform, and her general person. Finally, he returned the salute and invited her into his office. His aide followed them in, he glanced at Shenin and asked, "You drink coffee, lieutenant?"

"Yes, sir," Shenin answered.

"Two coffees," he told his aide. "You take cream, sugar?"

"Both, please," she said, smiling warmly at the aide, a younger woman.

The aide smiled back, and nodded. "Right away sir," she said.

"Have a seat," the captain said, smiling.

"Thank you, sir." Shenin said, sitting down, but still stiff at attention.

Chappy waved his hand dismissively. "At ease lieutenant, there are no generals in here."

Shenin relaxed, glad to note that he didn't seem to stand on ceremony.

"So you're here from Nellis, right?"

"Yes, sir." She nodded.

"You were part of that security unit that got shot at during the floods, weren't you?"

"I was the one that got shot initially," Shenin replied.

"Crazy shit, that," he said, shaking his head as he sat down at his desk. "Fortunately, we don't usually have that kind of excitement here. The last time we had to draw down on anyone, it was a moose intent on mating with one of the aircraft."

Shenin laughed. "I can see how that could be problematic," she said.

"You're sure as shit there," Chappy replied.

The aide returned with the coffee at that point. Once again she smiled warmly at Shenin, her eyes connecting an extra moment longer than necessary. Shenin was surprised by it. The one thing Tyler had told her about how she knew when someone was gay, her "gaydar," was when a woman held eye contact just a little longer than necessary. She reasoned that most people who weren't gay probably didn't know it, maybe it was the younger woman's way of finding out if she was gay. It was an interesting feeling.

"I'm gonna assign you to our younger unit here," Chappy was saying. "Thank you Anne," he said, dismissing the aide. "I think they'll appreciate your youth, and maybe it'll inspire some of them to becoming officers like you. I've heard really good things about you, Devereaux, your unit commander thought very highly of you."

"Thank you sir, that's good to hear," Shenin said, thinking that Teri was reaching out from Nellis and giving her a pat on the back.

They talked some logistics for another half hour, and then he dismissed her to go over to supply and get some cold weather gear. At supply, it seemed luck was with her, she got an incredibly nice supply officer, who was all too happy to issue her whatever she wanted.

"What will I need?" she asked. "I'm coming from Nellis in Vegas."

"That explains a lot," the older man said, grinning. "Okay I'm gonna suggest that you go with the Gore-Tex jacket and the fleece liner." He gave her a sidelong glance. "I'm going to guess a size four, on the shirt," he said.

"And I love you for saying that," she said, smiling, "but more like a six. I usually take a medium."

"Six is better, young'un," he said, winking at her. "What size boots?" he asked, leaning over the counter, "I'm guessing six and a half."

"You're guessing right," she replied.

She left the supply building with everything she was likely to need to stay warm. Walking outside, she found that once again, she had no idea how to get to officers' quarters. It reminded her of the day she'd met Tyler, which made her heart heavy suddenly. She sat down on a bench outside of supply, and just closed her eyes for a few moments. She knew that by this time, Tyler and the unit would be halfway to Iraq and she had no idea if Tyler had gotten her email or replied. Either way, she needed to get moving before she froze to death, she got up from the bench and looked around. Right about that time an older woman walked past. Shenin turned to her and was actually surprised when the women snapped to attention and saluted her. Shenin returned the salute sharply, then smiled at the woman.

"Can you help me?" she asked. "I need to figure out how to get to the officers' quarters, I just got here."

"Of course, ma'am," the woman replied instantly. "Officers' quarters are right down this road, on the left. Not too far of a walk, but a jeep would be better." With that, she whistled at an airman driving by in a jeep who immediately pulled over to the side of the street. Jumping out of the jeep, he also snapped to attention and saluted her. It was an absolutely surreal experience for Shenin.

It was a scene she ached to share with Tyler, so when she finally got to the officers' quarters and got settled, she immediately started typing an email to Tyler about the experience:

Okay, so weird, I just got here, and was on the street, lost as usual, and two separate people saluted me. I mean, I know, that's what you do to officers, but I guess I'm just not used to being the officer they're saluting. The woman was probably like ten years older than me, it felt really weird! I hope everything is going well over there, and you're being safe. Love your crazy newbie officer friend, Shen.

There had been no email from Tyler, but she decided then and there that regardless of an answer, she was going to share stories with her friend. It somehow made her feel like nothing had changed between them and Shenin could keep the feeling of a tenuous connection between them if she was writing Tyler.

The next day she got the opportunity to meet her new unit. Walking into the situation room, she heard the usual bantering going on, but the moment someone saw her, the call for attention was issued. It was even more surreal when a room of six men and women snapped to attention and saluted her. Shenin snapped to attention as well, returning their salute. She noted the surprised look on some faces, but also the nods from others. It was a sign of respect to them for her to come to attention as well. The first thing she wanted her people to know was that she respected them, it was important to her.

"At ease," she said, smiling at all of them. "Good morning," she said, moving to stand at the front of the room. "As some or all of you may know, I'm Shenin Devereaux and I've been assigned as your commanding officer. First off, let me give you a little background on me. I'm originally from Sacramento, California and my first assignment as an airman was at Beale Air Force Base. I spent four years at Beale on the security force. My second assignment was Nellis Air Force Base, and I was part of the security force team there as well. I just finished my time at OTS, and this is my first command. Lucky you," she said, smiling on the last. There were chuckles from the group. "So, with that said, I want all of you to know that I know I'm new at this commanding thing, and as such, I am capable of making a mistake or two… or two hundred. If I do make a mistake, I would appreciate a heads up; just remember that if you treat me with respect, I will treat you the same way. I am a very casual person, regulations are regulations, but I know there is a time and a place for everything. Now, first off, do any of you have any questions for me, about me, or anything?"

A young woman in the front raised her hand slightly. "Ma'am, can you tell us what your expectations are for the unit?"

Shenin nodded. "Yes, the first thing I'll be doing is reviewing the training plan for the unit. I want to focus our energies in areas that need work. I'm going to be reading up on incident reports and general base reports to determine where I think those problems lie."

"Wildlife," someone piped up, making everyone laugh. "Sorry, ma'am," the voice said, immediately, sounding contrite.

"No worries, airman," Shenin said, grinning, "I hear the moose mating season here is rather dicey."

That had the whole group laughing.

"Any other questions?" she asked, looking around the room. When no one else spoke up, she nodded. "Okay, what I'd like to do next is talk to each of you individually. I want to get some background on all of you, and to get to know you. If you have any concerns, problems or suggestions, I'd be happy to listen to them now." Picking up the list in front of her, she called the first name on the list, "Aims?"

A young man stood up. "Ma'am," he said.

Shenin gestured to an anteroom of the squad room. He preceded her, waiting inside the room at attention until she got into the room. "At ease, Aims, have a seat."

The man was probably nineteen, and from what she could see, he was probably a former football hero, he had a strong build, and the tough guy look about him.

"Where are you from, Aims, John isn't it?" she asked, reading from the file in front of her.

"Yes ma'am, it's John. I'm from Arizona, ma'am, Tucson."

"How long have you been in?"

"Just got here a month ago ma'am, basic training before that," he replied.

Shenin nodded. "Oh good, we'll have our first winter here together," she said, smiling, doing her best to put him at ease.

"Why'd you join?" she asked.

"I wanted to serve my country, ma'am," he replied, with what she considered a canned answer.

Shenin nodded, wanting to crack his formal exterior.

"The GI Bill to pay for school didn't appeal to you?" she asked, grinning. "Or did they tell you that you'd get to travel to exotic locations?"

It took him a long moment, but he started to grin. "Second one, ma'am, I wasn't ready for college yet."

"So you like moose?" she asked, smiling now.

He laughed outright at that. "No, ma'am, but I'm thinking they might be good eating."

That had Shenin laughing and nodding. "Or at least a good coat, right? So, do you have any concerns for the unit, or your job here?"

John thought for a moment, obviously hesitating.

"John, this is between you and me, you can tell me anything, okay?" she told him. "I'm here to help you, I mean that."

"Honestly ma'am, the ASVAB test said I had the aptitude for security force but I'm just not sure. I've honestly never held a gun in my life before basic training."

The ASVAB test was supposed to determine what kind of job someone would be suited to when first joining the military. However, in this case, it hadn't seemed to have worked so well.

"Tech school didn't help with any of that?" Shenin asked.

"I made it through," John said, "but I barely made it, and I still feel like I'm all thumbs. I just don't feel like I can protect my fellow airmen."

Shenin nodded, understanding his fear. "Okay, well, we can certainly get you more training with weapons, if that's what you want to do. Do you feel like you shouldn't be in security?"

"I don't really know ma'am, so far it's been okay, but I just don't know how I'm going to react when the shit hits the fan, you know?" His eyes widened suddenly as he realized he'd just cussed in front of an officer. "Oh, ma'am, I'm sorry," he began, looking terrified.

Shenin grinned. "Relax airman, I can cuss with the best of them, don't worry about it. Okay, so what I think we need to do is do some situational training. We can evaluate your reaction time, and your performance. Once we run through some of this and work with you on weapons, we can revisit the issue, okay? If you really get to feeling like you can't do this, I will be more than happy to help you transfer. Does that work for you?"

The young man smiled like it was Christmas morning. "Yes, ma'am, thank you."

"We'll get through this together, okay?" Shenin said, standing up and putting out her hand.

John stood as well and grasped her hand, smiling and nodding his head. "Yes ma'am."

"My door is open any time in the meantime," Shenin added. "Can you send in Cannel, next?" she asked him.

"Will do, lieutenant." He turned and left, the young woman who'd asked the question in the briefing entered the room next. She immediately snapped to attention, saluting, Shenin returned the salute.

"Airman 1st Class Cannel," Shenin said, glancing at her list. "At ease, have a seat."

The young woman sat down. Shenin had read that she was twenty-three.

"It's Gina, right?" Shenin asked.

"Yes, ma'am," the girl responded.

"From San Diego, huh?" Shenin asked.

"Yes, ma'am, born and raised."

Shenin nodded. "I was there on vacation a few times," she said. "It's nice."

"Yeah? Try living in the poor part of town," Gina responded snidely, and then realized who she was talking to. "Oh, ma'am, sorry," she said chagrinned.

"Don't worry about it Cannel, I get that, trust me. So tell me a little bit about yourself."

"I grew up without a dad, but my mom did her best for me and my three brothers. I'm the oldest," she said. "I figured joining the Air Force was the only way I was going to get to see the world."

Shenin nodded. "I can understand that. What are your plans while you're in?"

Gina looked unsure of herself. "I've been in for four years," she said, "I'm not sure I really have a plan."

"Any college?" Shenin asked.

"Yeah, I got my associates," Gina answered. "Why?"

"Just wondered if you were interested in becoming an officer," Shenin asked, thinking about what the captain had said about influencing her young team.

Gina looked surprised by the question. "I'm not officer material ma'am," she said, shaking her head.

"What makes you say that?"

Gina shrugged. "I'm not smart like that."

"I'm not sure that's true, Airman Cannel, the question you asked in the briefing was good, it was with an eye to the future."

"I just wanted to know what we were in for." Gina grinned.

"That's what leaders want to know," Shenin said. "Look, I'm with you, I grew up without a father, my mom trying to raise me and my brother. I joined the Air Force because I was tired of men telling me what 'us' little girls couldn't do. I became security force for the same reason," she said, her look direct, "I became an officer, because I wanted some say over what happened in my unit."

Gina considered then she looked back at Shenin and asked, "Do you think I could really do it?"

"I think if it's something you think you want to do, you should start working toward it."

"But how would I do the school stuff?"

"Do it like I did," Shenin said, "online. It'll maybe take you two years, shorter time if you do a private program, but we could look into it for you, if you're interested."

"I'll definitely think about it, ma'am," Gina said, thinking that this new LT was pretty cool.

"Good, let me know what you decide, and I'll help you in any way I can," Shenin said, smiling. "Now, last thing, are there any problems or concerns you see with the unit? Or do you have any suggestions for me?"

"We got a really good unit here," Gina said. "I mean, Aims is pretty new, and pretty green, but I think he could really work out with the right kind of push. Green is kind of a jerk sometimes, but I think he does it just to get a rise out of people. I think our biggest problem right now is the boredom and the lack of training."

Shenin nodded. "Good assessment, see? Leadership," she said, winking. Gina chuckled.

The next few interviews went smoothly, not too many had much to say. Shenin figured it was probably that they weren't sure about her yet. She made a note to touch bases with everyone again in a month or so to get some feedback from them all again. Her last interview was with David Green, Airman 1st Class.

"So, Green," Shenin said. "Your file says you've been in for ten years."

"Yes, ma'am," he said, nodding. He was nice looking, but Shenin sensed that he thought he was better looking than he was, it was in the way he carried himself.

"And you've been security force the whole time?"

"Yeah," David said, looking at his fingernails critically. "I wanted to go into the Marines, but I decided the Force needed me more."

Wow, Shenin thought, *no ego there.* To David she said, "I see and what do you feel that you bring to the table here?"

"Well, it is, me," he said, with what Shenin assumed was his most charming smile.

In response, she gave him a tight smile, and continued to wait in silence for an actual answer. The silence stretched for a full minute, before he suddenly seemed to get the message that she was still waiting for an answer and didn't find him as charming as he thought he was.

"Well, I am a good marksman, I've gotten two seventy-five on the range a lot of times. I also have a law enforcement background."

Shenin nodded, not looking the least bit impressed; she'd read about his "law enforcement background." He'd been a dispatcher for a security company for a year before he joined the Air Force. And she got three hundred, a perfect score, on the range every time, except for right after she'd been shot in the shoulder, and even then it had still been two ninety. He was full of himself for no truly good reason.

"What are your goals, Green?" she asked, her tone not friendly, she knew she needed him to understand that the way he was acting was not acceptable to her, so he'd adjust his approach.

"I want to make NCO," he said quickly.

"What are you doing to accomplish that?" Shenin nodded, thinking that this airman had a lot of work to do to become the supervisor level of Non-Commissioned Officer.

David seemed taken aback by the question. "Ma'am?" he queried.

"Time served, doesn't earn you NCO, airman," Shenin said. "You have to work for it. What have you done to move toward your goal?"

"I..." he stammered, "well, I really haven't, but I just figured..." his voice trailed off, and Shenin could see his ego was slightly deflated now.

Clearing her throat, she said, "What I'd like to see from you Green is how you work with your team, how you interact them. I'll evaluate you, and give you some feedback as to what I think you can do to move toward NCO, okay? But first we have to work on getting you up to senior airman, you have the time in service, I just need to help you figure out what's holding you back. Are you willing to work with me on this?"

David looked back at her, surprised by her question. It started occurring to him that he may have been shooting himself in the foot for a while with his ego games. He finally nodded, knowing that he needed to be careful now. This woman was new to being an officer, but obviously not new to being a leader, she also didn't seem like she would take much shit from him.

That night she settled in with some files to read and a cup of strong coffee. Before she started to read, she tapped out a quick email to Tyler again:

Had my first unit meeting today. Couple of standouts in the group. One kid who is terrified to be on the security force, because he doesn't know if he can handle it when he gets in the shit, and a girl that I can see becoming an officer one day if she believes she can. I think this might be a good situation here. I miss you like crazy, and I hope you're being safe. Thinking about you a lot. Love, Shen.

CHAPTER 6

Tyler looked around the base, taking in the subway and the movie theater. *Rough gig this being deployed stuff,* she thought wryly to herself knowing all the while that it could be every bit as dangerous as it was homey. They were there to help the Air Force clear out the base known as Joint Base Balad or Mortaritaville as many airmen and other soldiers called it, due to the high level of mortars that had been lobbed at the base. The base had been the logistical hub for the Air Force in Iraq for many years, and it housed the Air Force Theater hospital, which had a 98 percent survival rate for the soldiers who'd been sent there when injured. However, the Air Force was pulling out, and naturally that was causing more chaos with terrorists, not less. It was Terri and her unit's job to secure the base and investigate anything suspicious.

"Enjoy the view now, ladies," the commanding officer they'd been greeted by was telling them, almost as if reading Tyler's thoughts as she stood at attention. "This will all be going away in the next few months as we shut down. By the time we're done here in November, we're going to be in tents and eating MREs, so enjoy it while it lasts." He was referring to the long lasting, packaged Meals Ready to Eat that military troops had to rely on in the absence of dining facilities. Not exactly a favorite amongst the team, but they were better than nothing.

Tyler kept the grin off her face, but inside she was thinking, *see dumbass, that's what you get for being cocky.*

Later in the air conditioned huts set up for the airmen, Sheila laughed and said, "MREs? I'm gonna fuckin' die!"

"We'll all lose those pesky last five pounds, that's for sure," Jean said, grinning.

"Speak for yourself," Sheila said, laughing.

"I was!" Jean said.

Tyler shook her head, lying back in her bunk and closing her eyes. They'd been up for over forty-eight hours, since they'd received their orders, packed their gear and the items they'd need for the time in Iraq, and then the sixteen hour plane ride. She was too tired to get involved with the game. Closing her eyes, she felt herself sink lower into the bunk and was asleep a moment later.

The last couple of months had been really hard for her. It was crazy how much someone could come to mean to a person in such a short time. She'd been friends with Shenin for less than a year, but having no communication with her was weighing so heavily on her. Sheila and Jean saw it, and hated that things had somehow gotten screwed up between the two women, and they really hated to see their friend so dismal. They were doing everything they could think of to keep her spirits up.

"Did you hear back from Dev?" Jean asked, knowing that Sheila had emailed Shenin when they'd found out they were being deployed.

"Haven't even gotten a chance to check. I'll have to charge my phone to see if I can check for it here," Sheila said. "If not I'll get to the admin building and check it from a hard connection."

It was another two weeks before anyone had time to think of emails from home. Sheila finally was able to check her email from a hard connection in the admin building. She told Jean about Shenin's email, but since she hadn't specifically mentioned Ty, Sheila was loath to say anything to Tyler.

Back in Alaska, Shenin found herself emailing Tyler all the time, just telling her about things that happened during the day. She was careful keeping her emails 'safe,' since she was using Tyler's Air Force email account. After two months, Tyler still hadn't answered. Shenin was beginning to think she was never going to talk to her friend again. Finally she broke down and emailed Sheila again to get an update on her friend:

Hey, Sheila, me again. How are things going over there? Is everyone doing alright? Okay, yeah, I want to know how Tyler is doing specifically. Is she getting any of my emails? I'm sorry to put you in the middle of this, but I miss my friend. Stay safe over there. Dev.

Three days later, when Shenin checked her email, she was beyond thrilled. Tyler had answered every one of her emails, the last of which was in response to the first email she'd sent before they'd been deployed. Her email was equally careful:

Sorry it took me so long to get to this email, I didn't even think to check my emails. No one ever writes me on them! My parents don't even own a computer! As for how we left things, I'm sorry too. I just care about your well-being too much to let you make that bad decision. But I could have handled it better. We are being careful over here, not to worry.

On another note, I got a personal email address today, and I even bought an iPhone so I can get personal emails. Here's the address hrlywmn@yahoo.com write me there when you get a chance.

Shenin bit her lip. That was code for, *They watch our mail here, so if you want to say something you don't want to take that chance that the Air Force will read, then write my private address.* She immediately grabbed her personal phone and using her own personal email address sent Tyler another message:

Message received! I've missed you so much! You better be telling me the truth about being careful! I'll kick your ass if you're not! I can't believe you're so far away, I feel like we're on different planets right now, and I hate it! Send me pictures of where you guys are, is it top secret, or can you tell me where you're at and what you're doing? Details if you can please! Love, Shen.

She hit send on the email feeling alive for the first time in months. She had her friend back and it was an amazing feeling!

That night when she got home, she found that she had another email from Tyler, from the private email.

I promise you that we are being careful. Attached is a picture of the girls and me in our little hut that apparently is going to end up being a f'ing tent in the next couple of months! We're at Joint

Base Balad, helping to close it up, nothing really exciting. I think the most danger we're probably in is either dying from boredom, or sunburn. Sounds like you have your hands full with those pups, but I know you'll be amazing and they're lucky to have you for a CO. Don't work too hard over there. Love you, and miss you. Ty.

Shenin wondered, was it crazy that she focused on the "love you" part of the email? Did she mean that? Well, sure, she meant it, but did she mean it as her friend or romantically? Shenin banged her head lightly with the phone.

She began getting daily emails from Tyler, and she naturally answered them all. It became the highlight of her day.

Things with her unit were progressing nicely. Aims was improving his weapons skills consistently. The unit was set to start situational drills the following week. Even Gina had told her that she'd looked into some online programs and was seriously thinking about giving it a shot. In the meantime, Shenin had found that once Green's ego had been taken down a peg or two, he was actually a nice guy. She did her best to help him understand the difference between ego and confidence and it seemed to be helping.

One afternoon they'd just taken a break for lunch when Shenin's cell phone rang. When she looked at the screen it said unknown caller, but she went ahead and answered anyway, thinking she could hang up on any telemarketer.

"Hello?" she answered.

She was greeted with, "What're you doin'?" She was sure she'd never been so happy to hear a person's voice in her whole life.

"Hi!" she enthused. "What're you doin'?" she mimicked. "It's probably more interesting than me anyway," she said, walking around the end of a building, and moving to sit on a barrel. It was cold, and snowing, but she didn't notice any of that.

"Oh, it's midnight here, so I'm lying here in my bunk, staring up at the ceiling."

"You do lead the life," Shenin said, grinning.

"I know, right?" Tyler agreed, laughing.

"So how is it going over there?" Shenin asked. "How much longer do they expect you to be there?"

"They figure we'll be here till around next November."

"Ugh, that long, huh?"

"Yeah," Tyler said. "So I must not have interrupted you, since you answered the phone, what are you up to?"

"We just broke for lunch. We're doing situational drills, exciting stuff," Shenin said, grinning, absolutely thrilled to be talking to Tyler again.

"Uh-huh, figured it would be just about lunchtime there," Tyler said.

"Of course you did," Shenin said, ever amazed that her friend took into account things like that.

"So..." Tyler said, grinning with blue eyes twinkling mischievously on the other end of the line, "what're you wearing?" she asked, making it sound like a suddenly obscene phone call.

Shenin laughed out loud, startling someone walking by She held up her hand and mouthed "Sorry," to the passerby.

"I'm wearing BDUs and a parka..." she said, her voice low and sexy.

"Oh, so hot..." Tyler said, laughing on her end. "How cold is it there now?"

"Oh, I think we might get over zero today, then again, it is snowing right now."

"Wow," Tyler said, shaking her head. "I bet you look cute in your parka and boots."

"Oh, I do, trust me, I'll send you a picture, I kind of look like a cammo Michelin man."

Tyler laughed at that picture.

A jeep rumbled by Shenin's perch.

"You aren't sitting outside, are you?" Tyler asked.

"Uh," Shenin said, "yeah, kinda."

"Is there a roof over your head?" Tyler asked mildly.

Shenin looked up. "Well, no, but I'm next to a building."

"You are crazy, woman, you said it's snowing."

"I wanted to be able to talk to you more freely," Shenin said, looking around her again.

Tyler was silent for a moment. "I missed you too, Shen," she said finally, her tone so warm and so soft that Shenin found herself gripping the phone tighter. Tears stung the backs of her eyelids. She couldn't help the resulting sniffle. "Don't cry," Tyler said, knowing her well enough to know that the sniffle had nothing to do with the snow and cold.

"I know," Shenin said, as more tears welled up in her eyes. Swallowing convulsively she said, "I miss you so much."

On her end, Tyler closed her eyes, she knew she was walking on a dangerous edge at that moment, but she felt so far from home, and so far from someone who meant so much to her. She would give anything to reach through the phone and touch her face, wipe away her tears. Sometimes she really, really hated the Air Force and this was one of those times.

"Tyler?" Shenin queried when there was a long silence.

"I'm here," Tyler said softly. "Right here."

"I really wish you were," Shenin said.

"Me too," Tyler replied, sighing she glanced at her watch. "I better go, or this call is going to cost me a month's pay."

"Call collect next time," Shenin said.

"Like hell I will," Tyler replied. "But I will call, okay?"

Shenin shook her head at Tyler's stubborn reply. "Okay," she said, not willing to argue the point of who paid for a call. "Please stay safe, Tyler."

"You too," Tyler said, and then she said it, "love you."

Shenin closed her eyes, letting the sound of those words smooth over her, it wasn't "I love you", but it was enough. "Love you, Ty," she responded, making Tyler sigh softly on the other end.

"Bye for now," Tyler said, after another long pause, as if she was loath to say it, and she was.

"Talk to you soon," Shenin said, emphasizing the word soon.

They hung up; it was only then that Shenin realized Gina was standing a foot away from her, obviously waiting to talk to her. There was that moment of fear, what had the girl overheard, could she hear what Tyler had said too? Suddenly Shenin experienced the fear that she imagined many gays in the military experienced regularly.

As soon as Shenin looked at her, the girl snapped a salute. "Sorry, ma'am, I didn't mean to eavesdrop," Gina said, looking contrite.

Shenin returned the salute. "It's okay, it was my best friend, she's over in Iraq right now," Shenin said.

"Is she military?" Gina asked.

"She's Air Force too, she was part of my old unit at Nellis," Shenin told her, it somehow felt good to talk about Tyler for a second, like they hadn't just hung up. "Anyway, did you need something?"

"I was just going to tell you that I got word today that I got into that online program I applied for," Gina said, smiling.

"Really?!" Shenin enthused. "That's great! Now this is the one that will work with you on paying for college, right? So you're not out of pocket?"

"Yes, ma'am, that's the one," Gina said, happy that her Commanding Officer seemed to be in touch with her people and what they were doing.

"That is awesome, Gina, it really is, I'm really happy for you. I think this is going to be the start of something really big for you," Shenin said, honestly.

"I hope so ma'am," Gina said, smiling.

It was a good day, made even better by an email from Tyler that night.

Hated to hang up, today. Felt like old times for a bit there, I miss those times, but I guess we have to move forward, huh? Don't forget my picture of the high fashion parka, gotta have something to chuckle at. Love you, Tyler.

Shenin decided to take a series of pictures for Tyler so show her what she saw every day. First, she took a picture of her parka and boots sitting on the bed; then she took a picture of her bathroom; and then of her in her BDUs, parka, liner and boots, hood on, hood off, looking silly. Next, she took a picture of the car she'd bought herself upon arriving at Eielson: a Spring Special Blue 2010 Dodge Challenger SRT 8 Mopar edition. She knew that Tyler would get a kick out of the car, since they'd talked about how awesome the new version of the old classic was. She then took pictures on the way to the squad rooms. She talked to her squad and asked them if they'd be willing to take some pictures with her to send to her best friend. They were all willing to do that. She'd become pretty close to her squad. They sensed that she respected them, and that made the feeling mutual. In the end, Shenin spent hours sending each picture with a caption to tell Tyler what was what.

She got an email in response to the pictures.

These were absolutely awesome, Shen, thank you! I almost feel like I'm there! Keep an eye on your phone, for the Iraq edition. Love you, oh and LOVE, LOVE, LOVE the car! You did it! Ty.

Shenin could barely wait to get the pictures. The pictures she got were very different however, because there were a lot involving Tyler, Sheila and Jean all wearing their battle dress uniforms, with their M-16s and all their other battle gear on. It actually made her a little nervous, but she knew that wasn't Tyler's intent, so she kept her mouth shut about that. There were pictures of the three of them at the subway on base, and even at the McDonald's there too. Tyler even took a selfie with her lying in her bunk, her bright blue eyes were so soft, Shenin could almost feel them looking at her. She loved the picture instantly and saved it as her wallpaper on her phone. She knew it was a dangerous thing to do, but that picture couldn't get filed away with the others, it was too meaningful.

In response, she took a selfie of herself sitting outside on the one nice day they'd had in the last month, where the sun was actually shining. She sent it to Tyler, with a smiley face and the words, "OMG it's the sun!"

Tyler was just dropping off to sleep when her phone dinged, which meant she'd gotten an email. Shenin was the only person emailing that account, so she had to check it, and when she opened the picture she was so glad she did. The picture of Shenin captured everything that was gorgeous about the woman, including her gold colored eyes. The sun was shining in the background and Shenin's eyes seemed to almost glow as she looked directly at the camera. Tyler felt a very visceral reaction to the picture, and was reminded once again why she was in love with this girl, Christ she was beautiful. It dragged at her again, that this could never be, they could never be together openly. Especially now that Shenin was an officer, it put up one more obstacle: they couldn't even really hang out without raising all kind of regulatory red flags. It sucked… it sucked so much that Tyler had to suppress the urge to scream. Instead she stared at the picture of Shenin, and felt her heart break a little bit more. There was a lump in her throat suddenly, and she felt tears pushing to the surface. Tyler fell asleep that night with the phone cradled against her, and tears on her cheeks.

The next day Shenin got an email back in response to the picture.

Picture killed me, God you are beautiful. Love you, Ty.

Shenin had her own physical reaction to those words and like Tyler, her heart broke a little bit.

The emails continued back and forth, but they were much less intense. It was as if each of them realized they were just hurting themselves by heading down that path, even via the internet. But calls still tended to be more intimate.

The second time Tyler called Shenin, she caught her just as she was waking up for the day.

"What're you doin'?" came the familiar question.

"Lying here in bed," Shenin replied simply, grinning.

"That's just plain evil," Tyler said, narrowing her eyes on the other end.

"Why?" Shenin asked, thinking she might know why, but curious as to whether Tyler would admit to it.

"Shenin Doaha Devereaux, you know damned good and well why," Tyler said, her tone a bit husky.

Shenin shivered at the sound of Tyler's voice. "Do I?" she asked, teasing.

"Should I ask what you're wearing?" Tyler countered.

"You might not like the answer," Shenin replied.

"Why?"

"'Cause I'm naked," Shenin replied, and heard Tyler immediately suck in her breath on the other side of the world.

"You're just wrong…" Tyler said, shaking her head on the other end.

"You asked, darlin'," Shenin drawled.

"Yeah, and now I'm going to have a hard time thinking straight the rest of the day," Tyler replied.

"Can you do that?" Shenin asked, grinning again.

"Do what?"

"Think *straight*," Shenin said, her voice emphasizing the word straight.

Tyler burst out laughing. "Cute," she said, smiling.

"I am, sometimes, aren't I?" Shenin said.

Tyler cleared her throat, "More than," she said, thinking back to the picture.

"So you liked my picture?" Shenin asked.

"A lot," Tyler said.

"I really loved the one you sent me, that's why I had to do one for you."

"Well, I'm glad you did, it made my night and a number of days since then," Tyler told her.

"I love that about you," Shenin said.

"What?" Tyler asked.

"That you'll tell me what you're thinking, that you'll tell me how you really feel about things, and me. You're so honest, it's a wonderful thing, Ty."

Tyler smiled fondly. "And I love that you say stuff like that," she said.

They were both quiet for a minute, each lost in their own thoughts.

"Busy day today?" Tyler asked.

"Nope, off today. So I'm going to eat breakfast and then hit the gym, for cardio dance."

"What's a cardio dance?" Tyler asked.

"Cardio dance, it's an exercise class," Shenin said, grinning. "One of my people told me about it."

"Okay, so what is it?"

"It's kind of a cross between Latin and hip hop dance," Shenin said.

"Sounds like something I'd like to see," Tyler said.

"You can probably Google it," Shenin said.

"No," Tyler said. "It's something I'd like to see you doing," she said, emphasizing the word "you".

"Yeah… I don't think so," Shenin said.

"Don't be like that," Tyler said, her grin evident.

"I am not going to send you video of me sweating and looking dopey!" Shenin insisted.

"Don't make me pull strings…" Tyler said, her voice trailing off.

"You have strings in Fairbanks, Alaska?" Shenin asked.

"I have strings everywhere, babe," Tyler said confidently.

CHAPTER 7

Shenin found out later that week what strings Tyler had at the Eielson Air Base. There was a knock on her door a couple of hours after she got back from the gym one day. She was cleaning so she answered the door with a cleaning cloth and polish in her hand. She was surprised to see the captain's aide standing at her door, she thought she was being called in on her day off.

"Hi," she said, realizing that she couldn't remember the woman's name.

"My name is Anne," she told Shenin.

"It's nice to actually meet you," Shenin said. "Would you like to come in?"

"Yes, ma'am," Anne answered.

Shenin opened the door welcoming her into the apartment. Anne looked around, smiling.

"So, what can I do for you?" Shenin asked.

"I've been asked to do a favor for a mutual friend," Anne said, grinning.

Shenin looked back at her for a long moment. "Would this mutual friend be located in Iraq currently?" Shenin asked.

"One in the same," Anne said, grinning.

Shenin realized she'd been right about the captain's aide, and then it occurred to her.

"How do you know, Tyler?" She asked.

"Well," Anne began, "we first met in basic training. And then I was stationed at Nellis a few years later…" her voice trailed off.

"After," Shenin said, indicating after Tyler found out she was gay.

"Yes," Anne said, nodding.

"So you two dated," Shenin said.

"Yeah," Anne confirmed.

"Maybe we should sit down," Shenin said, gesturing to her couch. "Do you want some coffee?"

"That would be great," Anne said, smiling.

A little while later, they both had coffee and Shenin couldn't help but ask questions.

"So, you and Tyler… how was that?"

Anne looked circumspect for a moment, not sure what Shenin would want to hear, but the woman had asked.

"It was good," Anne said, nodding, "but I think I was a little too plain Jane for her."

Shenin looked confused. "How so?"

"Well, you know Tyler, she's pretty smart, and she's not your average woman, I just really couldn't keep up with her. I don't know how much you know about her, she said you're straight, but Tyler would kind of be considered a rock star in the lesbian community."

"Rock star?" Shenin asked.

"Everyone wants a piece of her," Anne explained.

"Now that doesn't surprise me at all," Shenin said, knowing how Tyler was, and imagining that she wasn't the first woman to think that Tyler would be the most incredible person in the world to date.

"Yeah, Tyler's a bit different from a lot of lesbians in the military community. I think the fact that she doesn't put up with a lot of drama, and basically tells it like it is, makes her a hot commodity. Not to mention she's pretty hot all on her own."

Shenin suppressed a grin, this definitely sounded like the Tyler she knew.

"So," Anne began, "can I ask what the story is with you and Tyler?"

Shenin nodded. "Of course you can, since she involved you in this little plan of hers," she said, smiling. "I met her a year ago; we were on the same security force team. We've been friends since then."

"So you're not dating?" Anne asked, having gotten the distinct impression that Shenin Devereaux was really important to Tyler.

"I'd like to date her, but she won't do it," Shenin said.

"Because you're straight," Anne said, nodding.

"Why does everyone keep saying that, damnit! If I want to date her, how straight can I be? I just don't get this logic," Shenin said, feeling frustrated.

Anne grinned. "Look, something you need to know about Tyler, and other lesbians is that there are two kinds of lesbians when it comes to straight women."

"Okay..." Shenin said, "what types are there?"

"When it comes to sex with straight women, there are lesbians that are more than happy to add a notch to their belt to nail a straight woman; they'd do anything to get into a straight woman's pants, basically for the right to brag about it."

"That's not Tyler," Shenin said, her tone sure.

"You're right," Anne said, "that's not Tyler. Tyler is not into using women like that, and the last thing she wants to be for any straight woman is an experiment. You know, that whole "I kissed a girl" thing?" Anne said, referring to the Katy Perry song that talked about kissing a girl and hoping that her boyfriend won't mind it. "That line about not even knowing the girl's name and it just being a game to her?"

"I can understand that," Shenin said, nodding. "I wouldn't do that to her."

"Well," Anne said, "Tyler makes her mind up about something and that's usually it."

"She told me she wouldn't date me because she didn't want to ruin my life, or my career," Shenin said.

“That sounds like the Tyler I know,” Anne said, nodding.

Shenin sighed. “Yeah, it sucks.”

Anne reached over, touching Shenin’s hand. “I’m sorry.”

Shenin nodded, accepting the other woman’s consolation.

“So what does our dear friend Tyler want?” she asked finally, wanting to get on to a better topic.

“Well, she wants to see you doing that cardio dance thing,” Anne said, grinning.

“I knew it, that little shit!” Shenin said.

Anne laughed. “Give the woman a break, she’s in the friggin’ desert.”

“Oh, sure,” Shenin said, grinning, “she’s a big hero, so she should get to see me sweating and looking all yucky.”

“Exactly,” Anne said, laughing.

Shenin sighed. “Fine.”

“Oh good,” Anne said, “this way I can repay at least one of the favors I owe her.”

With that Anne and Shenin became fast friends. Tyler certainly got an earful the next time she called, however.

“Seriously?” Shenin said by way of answering her phone the next time Tyler called.

Tyler was already laughing.

"You made me do it," Tyler said, her tone accusing.

"Yeah, it's my fault," Shenin said, rolling her eyes on her end.

"Yes it is," Tyler countered, smiling. "Seriously though, I figured you could use a friend up there and Anne's a sweetheart."

"Who you dated," Shenin said.

"She told you that, huh?" Tyler said.

"Of course she did, but to be honest I guessed that and she just confirmed it. She tells me you're a bit of a rock star in the military lesbian community."

"Oh lord," Tyler said, now rolling her eyes. "Don't believe everything you hear."

"Uh-huh," Shenin murmured, knowing that Tyler had no ego about who she was, and would never believe for a second that she was anything but herself. "She definitely thinks you're awesome, though," Shenin continued, "and that makes her smart."

"It does, huh?" Tyler asked, grinning again.

"Yep," Shenin declared, "We're going to get you your video, by the way, but you damned well better reciprocate with something equally embarrassing."

Tyler laughed out loud at that, "I see," she said, "it's going to cost me, huh?"

"Yes ma'am it is," Shenin said.

"You got it, babe," Tyler said, once again making Shenin shiver.

"Do you know what that does to me?" she asked.

"What, what does?" Tyler asked, confused.

"You calling me babe the way you do," Shenin explained.

Tyler canted her head on her side of the conversation. "Honestly, no, it hadn't really occurred to me, but what does it do?"

Shenin smiled, shaking her head, of course she wouldn't have any idea how easily her words could affect someone, she was always just herself, never contrived, never scheming.

"Of course you wouldn't know," Shenin said. "Let's just say that it makes me all warm and fuzzy every time you say it."

"Warm and fuzzy, huh?" Tyler asked.

"Yep," Shenin confirmed.

"Good," Tyler said, "then I'll keep doing it."

"Like me all warm and fuzzy, do you?" Shenin asked, smiling.

"Frankly, yes," Tyler answered candidly.

Shenin sighed. "Anne also explained why you don't want to date me."

"And I thought I explained that," Tyler said.

"You said it's because of the military," Shenin said.

"And the fact that you're straight," Tyler added.

"Stop saying that!" Shenin said, narrowing her eyes. "Anyway," she said, emphasizing the fact that she was moving on with her statement, making Tyler grin at her end. "She said that other lesbians are all too happy to turn out a supposedly straight girl, but that's not you."

"Straight is accurate until it's proven that you're gay," Tyler put in.

"I swear to God if you don't stop saying that, I'll get on a plane to Iraq and come kick your damned ass," Shenin blazed.

Tyler's reaction was to chuckle. "I'm sorry, babe, but the fact is, you've only ever dated men, and you've only ever slept with men so that technically makes you straight not gay."

"And technically, I'm crazy about a lesbian who's as stubborn as a mule, and that's the only reason I've never dated a woman."

"Uh-huh," Tyler murmured from her end.

"You're gonna be the death of me yet, Hancock, I'm just telling you."

They hung up not too long after that. Shenin always felt so much happier after talking to Tyler. It kept her smiling a lot during the day.

"You look happy," Anne commented, they were shopping at the on base store.

"Talked to Ty this morning," Shenin said, really happy to have someone she could share this kind of information with. She realized that Tyler had been once again right, it was nice to have a friend, one who understood the situation, there in Alaska with her. She shook her head thinking, *score another one for the girl from Maryland*, Tyler was always looking out for her, even from six thousand miles away.

“Ah,” Anne said, feeling a little spike of jealousy, Tyler was by far the best woman she’d ever dated, but she knew they’d never been meant to be. It did definitely appear that Shenin was much more Tyler’s speed; she was the whole package. She truly hoped they could get it together.

A week later, Shenin came down with a cold, and had to stay in. She had been down for three days when she messaged her unit and asked one of them to come by to pick up some evaluation reports that were due. Gina was the one to show up.

Shenin answered her door. “Hi,” she said, smiling.

“Good morning, ma’am,” Gina replied.

Shenin opened the door wider, gesturing for Gina to enter. “Cannel, I’m in my pajamas, I think you could at least get away with calling me Shenin this morning.”

Gina relaxed visibly then. “Thank you,” she said, smiling. “You look like hell ma’… I mean, Shenin,” she said catching herself.

“Thanks, that makes me feel great,” Shenin said, rolling her eyes.

“Sorry,” Gina put in, grinning.

Shenin handed her a folder. “Thanks for this, just make sure they get reviewed by the team, and then signed and returned to me by tomorrow noon.” She gave the girl a direct look. “I can count on you for this, right?”

“Yes, ma’am, you can,” Gina insisted, forgetting and being more formal in her need to prove to Shenin that she was capable of handling this assignment.

"I believe you," Shenin said, nodding.

"Can I get you anything from the store, ma'am?" Gina asked. "Maybe some orange juice or cold medicine?"

Shenin started to say no, but her body said, *oh orange juice!* "Actually, that would be great," Shenin said, moving to her purse.

"I got it, ma'am," Gina said, holding up her hand to forestall Shenin from giving her money, "it's the least I can do for you." She smiled.

"Okay," Shenin said, accepting the other woman's generosity.

A half hour later when Gina returned, she knocked on the door.

"It's open," Shenin called from her couch, having started to feel worse again.

Gina walked in, seeing her lying on the couch. She pulled the orange juice out of the bag. "Do you want me to pour you some of this?" she asked, seeing that Shenin looked really weary.

Again, Shenin wanted to say no, but her body once again insisted that it wanted orange juice, but it had no intention of moving off the couch to retrieve it.

"That would be great," Shenin said, smiling weakly.

When Gina came back with the glass of orange juice, she set it down and looked down at her lieutenant critically, "Are you sure you shouldn't go to the infirmary?" Gina asked. "You look kind of grey."

Shenin shook her head. "No, I'm okay, I just need to rest. Thank you for all this," Shenin said, looking up at the other woman, "I really appreciate it."

Gina smiled looking almost shy at the praise, then she looked back at Shenin and smiled. "You're welcome, ma'am."

"Shenin, at least this morning," Shenin replied.

"Shenin," Gina repeated, furrowing her brow slightly like the name sounded foreign to her.

Gina left a few minutes later. An hour later, Tyler called and Shenin told her about how nice Gina had been.

Tyler was quiet for a moment, then asked, "She gay?"

"What?" Shenin replied, surprised by the question.

"Is she gay?" Tyler asked, her words measured and slower.

"No," Shenin answered instantly, "I mean, I don't think so. Why? What does that matter anyway? You know I don't have a problem with people being gay."

"I might have a problem with *that* one being gay," Tyler said.

"What? Why?" Shenin asked confused. "Ty?" Shenin queried when Tyler was silent for a long minute. "I don't even think she's gay, okay? I didn't get a vibe from her, the way I did Anne. Okay? Please don't worry."

Tyler nodded her head, having to mentally smack herself to get out of the spiral her mind was sending her on. "You're right, I'm sorry," she said. "I think the sun is baking my brain."

"So wear your cover more often," Shenin supplied, smiling.

"Uh-huh," Tyler murmured.

They talked for a while longer and then hung up.

Three weeks later, Shenin started to believe that Tyler was somehow omniscient. Anne had invited Shenin out with a group of her friends to a local gay bar called the Palace Theater. They'd been in the club for an hour when Shenin spotted Gina sitting with a small group of enlisted personnel.

"Son of a bitch..." Shenin muttered to no one in particular.

"What?" Anne asked, having heard her.

Shenin nodded in Gina's direction. "The one with dark hair in the middle is in my unit."

"Oh..." Anne said, thinking that she'd just outed another airman to an officer by bringing said officer to this club.

Shenin glanced at Anne and saw the stricken look on her face, "Anne, I'm not going to report her, Hell, I'm here, aren't I? It's just that Tyler asked me if she was gay, and I said I didn't think so, and here she was right. How does she do that?" she asked, shaking her head.

Anne laughed, shaking her head. "Gays know gays."

"Even ones they've never met?"

"Even those sometimes," Anne said, nodding.

Shenin stood up, looking in Gina's direction.

"Where are you going?" Anne asked.

"I'm going to go talk to her," Shenin said, "to make sure she knows she's safe." She added, to forestall the concerned look on Anne's face.

"Okay," Anne said, nodding.

Shenin made her way over to Gina, trying to decide what she was going to say. She didn't notice the looks she was getting along the way. Anne watched her go, wondering if the woman had any idea how much attention she was attracting. Shenin Devereaux was hot, with a body that wouldn't quit, and all that red hair and golden eyes. She was dressed in dark jeans, high-heeled boots and a sapphire blue shirt with a long black jacket that came to her mid-thigh. Her make-up was perfect and her hair was flowing past her shoulders in loose curls. The lesbians in the club were avidly watching this one.

Gina looked up just as Shenin got to the table she was sitting at. She stood up immediately, having to stop herself from saluting her lieutenant, but unable to keep the look of panic off her face.

"Let's talk," Shenin said, smiling at the younger girl.

Gina nodded, still looking terrified despite Shenin's smile.

They walked out of the club to a back patio that was relatively deserted, even though there were patio heaters on in every corner.

"Ma'am, I can explain," Gina began, her mind racing.

Shenin held up her hand to stop her.

"Gina, it's okay," Shenin said, her look direct.

Gina looked back at her for a long moment, her dark brown eyes showing both confusion and still a touch of fear.

Shenin reached out to touch the other girl on the shoulder, "It's really okay," she assured the girl.

"So, are you…?" Gina began to ask, then wondered if she shouldn't ask that question.

"Not according to my friends, no," Shenin replied wryly.

"Huh?" Gina asked, obviously confused by that statement.

"I've never dated a woman, or had sex with one," Shenin said breezily. "Apparently that makes me not gay."

Gina nodded slowly, her look saying, "Oh… kay…"

"I'm sorry," Shenin said. "I know I sound like a crazy person right now. Anyway, I just wanted you to be okay, and not worry that anything will get back to the base, it won't. As long as you're always appropriate on base, then you and I are good, okay?"

Gina nodded again. "Yes ma'am, thank you."

Shenin smiled, wondering if she was ever going to get the girl to call her Shenin regularly. Hell they were in a gay bar for God's sake.

They both went back inside then and began heading back toward their tables, when Gina turned around. "Can I buy you a drink, LT?" she asked, smiling.

Shenin nodded. "Sure," she said, following the girl to the bar.

A couple of shots later, Gina asked, "So who are you here with?"

Shenin nodded toward Anne and her friends.

"Oh," Gina said, looking unsurprised, "the captain's girl."

"She's a friend of a friend," Shenin explained.

"So, how come you've never dated a woman before? I mean, assuming you want to."

"It's complicated," Shenin said, not willing to get into that whole discussion with someone under her command. "But suffice it to say this realization is rather new."

Gina nodded understandingly then to Shenin's utter shock, she moved up very close, looking right into her eyes.

"I'd be happy to show you the ropes," Gina told her, her voice softer. "You know, like you did me."

Shenin's head came up as her eyes widened slightly, but she controlled her reaction, not wanting to undo her overall message of gay being okay with her. "I, uh..." Shenin began, as she eased back a bit, "thanks, but I've kind of got someone I'm involved with."

"But you said you weren't dating anyone..." Gina said, looking confused again.

"I'm not, she won't, it's complicated," Shenin said, stepping back to the bar and holding up two fingers to the bartender, who promptly winked at her. They were coming out of the woodwork in Shenin's mind.

The bartender put a double shot of tequila in front of her that Shenin slammed back quickly. Then she looked back at Gina, "I'm sorry, I guess I didn't really explain that originally."

"No, I'm sorry," Gina said, thinking she needed to stop drinking lest she make another fatal career mistake.

Shenin saw the look. "We're good," she said. "Okay? We really are."

Gina didn't look convinced. "I'm really flattered, I am," she assured the younger woman, "but this other woman's got me pretty caught."

Gina looked over at Anne, like she was trying to see it.

"Oh, no, not her," Shenin said, feeling the tequila hitting her suddenly. "She's in Iraq."

"Oh… your best friend," Gina said, remembering the conversation she'd overheard.

"Right," Shenin said, nodding.

"Well, you have a good night, LT," Gina said, wanting to escape at that moment.

"Have a good one," Shenin said, wanting the same thing.

Back at the table, Anne was all over her as she sat down with yet another double shot from the bartender who'd just told her that if she was interested she got off at two. Shenin was so busy reeling from the scene with Gina, she'd just nodded to the bartender, picked up her drink and walked away.

"What was that all about?" Anne asked, her eyes wide.

"She made a pass at me," Shenin said simply.

"Holy shit!" Anne said, laughing. "You are like the virgin at the prom, honey!"

Shenin sighed, shaking her head. "That's not funny," she said but started to laugh too. "Okay, it's a little funny."

"It's a lot funny!" Anne said, shoving at her shoulder.

Rhianna's 'S&M' came on at that point. Anne dragged Shenin out onto the dance floor with her and her friends and they danced, enjoying themselves. Shenin was completely unaware that half the bar was watching her dance, but Anne saw it, and thought Tyler was in deep shit if she didn't get back soon. And she told her so later that night.

"You need to come get your girl," Anne said to Tyler when she answered her phone at three pm in Baghdad. She noted that Anne sounded slightly intoxicated.

"I need to what?" Tyler asked.

"Come, get, your, girl," Anne repeated slowly.

Tyler cleared her throat, trying not to laugh outright. "I'm a little busy over here, Anne, so she's just going to have to wait."

"Yeah, well you might not have a girl anymore if you wait too long," Anne said.

"What's that mean?" Tyler said, becoming serious suddenly.

"We went out tonight to the club here," Anne said, "and every lesbian in the place was after her, including that chick from her unit."

Tyler went silent for a moment. "So she is gay," she said, her voice sounding somewhat defeated.

"Yeah, Shenin didn't know that though, she was really surprised to see the girl there."

Tyler nodded on her end. "Yeah, she didn't think she was."

"I'm telling you, my friend, your girl is a hot commodity, and if you want her, when you get back to the States, you better get your ass up here and do something about this once and for all."

Tyler sighed heavily, knowing Anne was right.

"Don't fucking take her back to that club, Anne, you got me?" Tyler said then, annoyed but knowing she was being irrational.

"And if she wants to go?" Anne said. "What am I supposed to do, forbid her?"

"Yeah," Tyler said, grinning, because she knew she sounded insane at the moment.

"Uh-huh," Anne said, pressing her lips together, "I'll just go ahead and order an officer not to go to a local club, we'll see how that goes over."

"You're not helping," Tyler said, grimacing.

"But I'm right," Anne said.

"Yes, you are," Tyler said, sighing again.

Tyler called Shenin the next morning, waking Shenin out of a dead sleep.

"Mmmm?" Shenin answered the phone, not even opening her eyes, she was hung-over that was for sure.

"Good morning, sunshine," Tyler said, smiling her at end.

"Hung-over, be nice," Shenin said, grinning.

"I'll try," Tyler said, softly.

"So you were right," Shenin said, wanting to get it over with quickly.

"About?" Tyler asked, already knowing the answer.

"About Gina, she's gay," Shenin said, her tone flat.

"Uh-huh," Tyler said, trying to contain her tone.

"Anne took me to the Palace Theater here, and I saw her there at the club. I talked to her to let her know I wasn't going to report her and—"

"She hit on you," Tyler added, unable to contain herself.

"What? Wait, how do you know that?" Shenin asked.

"Because Anne called me and told me," Tyler said.

"Really?" Shenin said, annoyed. "She didn't need to do that, I was going to tell you myself, if she's just going to tattle on me every time I—"

"She was calling me to tell me that I should get my shit together when it comes to you, Shen," Tyler interrupted again.

"Oh," Shenin said, losing her steam.

Tyler was quiet on her end for a moment and then she said, "I don't like it."

"Like what?" Shenin said, confused.

"That chick hitting on you," Tyler said.

"Why does it matter?" Shenin asked.

"Because she's hot, and she's there," Tyler answered simply.

"So?" Shenin said, still not sure what Tyler was trying to say.

On her end, Tyler did her best to tamp down on the jealousy that was slithering all around her heart at that moment. "I don't like it," she repeated stubbornly.

"Tyler, she's not into me, okay? And even if she is, I'm into one person, and that's you."

Tyler grimaced, knowing she was being beyond unfair, but she couldn't help it, the idea of this other woman getting to Shenin just twisted her into a knot. Swallowing convulsively, Tyler did her best to reign in her emotions that really wanted to come flying out of her mouth at that moment.

"Ty?" Shenin queried.

"I'm here," Tyler said, sighing. "I'm sorry, I just hate that I'm here, and you're there, and… and I'm so fucking stupid."

"You are not stupid," Shenin replied without hesitation.

"I am when it comes to you," Tyler said, her tone self-effacing.

"We'll figure this out, Tyler, somehow," Shenin said, even as she did, she knew it wasn't likely to get less complicated. She knew that even if Tyler would finally give up fighting the regulations/fraternization fight with her they'd still have an impossible task. No matter what, she was stationed in Alaska, and Tyler was stationed at Nellis, nothing was going to bring the two bases closer.

Tyler sat staring out over the sand, thinking along the same lines as Shenin. What would be the point in giving in? Either way they were far from each other. It wasn't fair to either of them to even start that up or continue the way they were now.

"I gotta go," Tyler said, feeling horrendously drained of all hope suddenly.

"Ty..." Shenin said, her voice beseeching.

"I just... I gotta go Shen, okay?" Tyler said, just wanting to go bury her head somewhere.

"Okay," Shenin said, closing her eyes slowly and feeling tears sting the back of them.

Tyler clicked off a moment later. Shenin lay on her bed crying for the next hour.

CHAPTER 8

Shenin didn't hear from Tyler over the next two weeks. She felt sick most of the time, but did everything she could to steel herself for the long haul. Once again she and Tyler were at odds, and she hated it more than anything in the entire world.

Her phone rang at two o'clock in the morning, two and a half weeks after the last time she'd spoken to Tyler. She was excited to think it was Tyler, but when she looked at the screen it said "Sheila" and before she even picked up she knew.

"Hello?" she answered.

"Dev, it's Sheila," the other woman said, her tone hurried. "Tyler's been hurt."

"Oh my God," Shenin said, feeling the world spin suddenly. "What happened, is she okay?"

"Fucking IED," Sheila said, Shenin could hear tears in her voice. "She heard it before it went off, and shoved Jean out of the way, it caught her in the chest..." Her voice broke off as she sobbed loudly.

"Sheila! Is she okay?" Shenin yelled, needing to know, but already terrified she did know.

"She's critical. They're trying to stabilize her here at the base hospital, if she makes it..." again she paused to take a shaky breath, "then they'll transfer her to Landstuhl Hospital in Germany. I'm sorry, Dev, I'm really sorry."

Shenin was crying, unable to think past that idea that Tyler could be dying at that very moment.

"I'm going to get there," Shenin said. "You text me when they transfer her, so I know where to go. Do you understand?"

Sheila nodded on the other end, but didn't answer.

"Sheila!" Shenin yelled. "You need to tell me that, you understand?"

"I understand, Dev," Sheila said, her voice sounding far away and haunted.

Shenin hung up the phone and then called Anne.

"Hello?" Anne mumbled.

"I need to get to Iraq, right now," Shenin ordered.

"Huh? What? Why?" Anne stammered.

"Tyler's been hurt, I need to get there, please help me," Shenin said, the tears starting again.

Within an hour, she was on a transport. It was going to take forever, but she was going to get to where she was needed. She just prayed to a God she didn't believe in that Tyler would still be alive when she got there. By the time the transport touched down at Joint Base Balad, Shenin had been traveling a full day with no sleep. She couldn't stop worrying about Tyler. Just after she landed at the base, she saw that Sheila had texted saying that they were evacuating Tyler to Landstuhl and to meet them there.

It was another eight hours to Landstuhl. She landed at Ramstein Air Base, and caught a jeep to the hospital. She'd been traveling for a day and a half at this point. Still, Shenin hit the front doors of the Landstuhl hospital at a dead run, looking for Sheila. She was directed to the ICU, where Sheila waited in the waiting room.

"Sheila!" Shenin called, running straight up to the other woman, hugging her. It was obvious Sheila had been crying. "How is she?"

Sheila took a deep breath, obviously trying to control herself

"She's in surgery right now," Sheila said. "She has a collapsed lung; she took a lot of shrapnel."

Shenin took a deep breath, blowing it out slowly, feeling nauseous and dizzy at the same time.

"Dev, she's in critical condition, they don't know if she's going to make it," Sheila said, looking completely stunned.

"She's going to make it," Shenin told her, her tone sure.

Sheila looked back at her for a long moment, but then nodded, knowing that Shenin needed to believe that in order to keep going.

"How's Jean?" Shenin asked.

"She's okay, she took a little bit of shrapnel, but she's going to be just fine. Ty saved her life," Sheila said.

"Always the hero," Shenin said, smiling fondly. Reaching out, she hugged Sheila, knowing the woman felt like hell for what was happening to her friend. "You should go get cleaned up, eat a meal and try to catch some sleep. I'll hang out here, and wait for word. Okay?"

Sheila looked like she wanted to argue, but finally nodded and headed off down the hall. Shenin moved to sit on a couch nearby. It was three hours before anyone came out to talk to her about Tyler.

"For Airman Hancock?" the doctor said, looking around.

Shenin stood up, and walked over to the doctor, "Lieutenant Devereaux, she's my area of responsibility," she said, hoping he didn't challenge her at this point.

The doctor nodded. "She's in recovery. We need to do more work on her, but her blood pressure dropped dangerously low, and she spiked a fever, so we didn't want to keep her under any longer. We managed to repair the damage to her lung and ascertain that there is no shrapnel threatening her heart. So we'll go back in when she's stronger to try and get more of the shrapnel. She's not out of the woods yet; I'm really concerned about the fever, so we're going to be watching her closely, I'm not willing to upgrade her status yet, I still consider her critical, we could still lose her. I'm very sorry."

Shenin stood listening to what he said, feeling completely numb.

"Is there any chance I can see her?" Shenin asked. "I've just flown a full day to get here and I only have so much leave. Sir, please…"

The doctor looked hesitant. "We're really not supposed to let anyone back there," he said, but he couldn't help but see how upset

Shenin was. "Yeah, go on back, she's in room thirty-seven. But don't stay too long."

"Thank you!" Shenin said, shaking his hand.

As she walked back to the recovery area, Shenin tried not to think about what she would do if she actually lost Tyler. There was no thinking beyond that, she couldn't imagine it. Walking into the darkened room, she could immediately hear the click and whir of machines. As her eyes adjusted to the dim light she saw Tyler lying in the hospital bed, it completely took her breath away. There were bandages covering her from her waist to her neck. There was a bandage on her head, even one on her cheek. Shenin closed her eyes, feeling sick again.

Gathering her strength she stepped forward, so she could look down at Tyler. She had to take deep breaths to overcome the desire to simply pass out from the sight she was beholding. This wasn't the Tyler she knew, this person was tiny, and hurt so badly, and not her Tyler at all. Sitting down in the chair near the bed, Shenin finally allowed herself to cry, leaning her head against the side of the bed she just let everything pour out of her. By the time she was done, she was exhausted. Keeping her head against the bed she listened to the machines make their noises, and let them lull her. She was asleep in minutes, exhausted.

She woke a few hours later feeling extremely stiff and with a major kink in her neck. Leaning up she looked at Tyler's face again, she even had bruising around both of her eyes. It was the worst thing she'd ever had to see and she was sure she was never going to lose that image. Standing up, she did her best to stretch and work out the kinks in her neck. Then she began pacing. Then she moved to the side of the bed where Tyler lay, still motionless, still unconscious.

"You have to be okay," she told her friend. "You have to be, that's all there is to it," She continued, nodding as if affirming what she was saying. "You can't leave me like this. That is just not going to happen, do you hear me Tyler? Do you?" She knew she sounded crazy, but part of her hoped that somehow Tyler could hear her, and somehow it would make her wake up and fight back.

It was another two days before Tyler even moved, even then she didn't wake up. Sheila had come back the next day and insisted that Shenin go and shower, sleep and get food.

"I'll shower, and get food," Shenin had said. "I can sleep right here. I need to be here if she wakes up."

Sheila hadn't been fool enough to argue with the feisty redhead. Tyler had finally started talking to Sheila about how she really felt about Shenin when they were in Iraq. It broke Sheila's heart for them that things just couldn't seem to work out. She knew Tyler was as stubborn as they came, and very adamant about not ruining Shenin's life by getting involved with her. The Air Force really was no place for gays, and it wasn't an easy thing to handle, and God help you if you were gay and fell in love with another member of the Air Force. You were simply doomed.

The third day that Shenin was at the hospital, she was sleeping with her head on the bed next to Tyler's leg. She woke to the sensation of fingers in her hair. Raising her head slowly, she looked up to see the most beautiful set of blue eyes looking down at her.

“Hi,” she whispered, her smile as bright as sunshine, tears instantly in her eyes.

Tyler pressed her lips together, trying to hold back her own tears at seeing her friend there. She had impressions of what had happened, she knew she’d been badly hurt and it was hard to breathe at that moment. She hurt everywhere, so much so that she couldn’t even pin point where.

“You’re… here,” Tyler managed, her voice raspy and weak.

“Where else would I be?” Shenin said, reaching out to take Tyler’s hand in hers gently. “My best friend in the entire world got hurt saving someone else’s life, where else would I go?”

“Jean?” Tyler asked in a hushed tone.

“Jean, is fine,” Shenin said, her tone strong. “Thanks to you.”

Tyler closed her eyes, nodding her head slightly. She squeezed Shenin’s hand, and Shenin saw a tear escape the corner of her eye and slip down her face. Shenin gently squeezed her hand in response. Then it was obvious that Tyler was unconscious again. Shenin found herself inexplicably thrilled for the few words Tyler had spoken. She was excited to tell Sheila when she got back from the cafeteria, bringing them both lunch.

“How much longer are you going to be able to stay over here?” Sheila asked, knowing that Shenin was on an emergency leave, and that was really pushing it since it wasn’t for a family member or spouse.

Shenin grimaced, not wanting to think about that at that point. She shook her head. "Not a lot longer," she said, her eyes on Tyler again, "but I'll stay until the very last minute that I can."

Sheila nodded her head, understanding the sentiment. Because Tyler was part of her unit, and forward command felt she would be helpful in Tyler's recovery, she'd been given permission to stay with Tyler. Shenin didn't have that same privilege, chances were when her commander figured out she was technically just visiting a friend, he was going to yank her leave, and she'd be in trouble. It was a risk and Sheila knew it. She was also extremely happy that Shenin was there, she knew it was what Tyler would need to fight this battle, Sheila just hoped that Tyler would be awake to see her for more than a couple of minutes.

As it turned out, Tyler only awoke one more time before Shenin had to leave. When she did wake up, Shenin was down the hall getting water, Sheila greeted her.

"Ty," Sheila said, smiling down at her friend, "Dev'll be right back, you need to try to stay awake, okay? She's gotta leave today, she's already been here four days, and her commander is hot right now. So please try to stay awake, just wait, please wait."

Tyler nodded slowly, looking like even that was a major effort.

Sheila ran over to the door, throwing it open, yelling at the top of her lungs, "Dev, get in here! She's awake!"

Shenin came at a dead run, knowing that the entire ward was looking at her like she was insane.

She skidded to a halt at Tyler's bed. She was dressed in her battle dress uniform, and to Tyler she was the most beautiful thing she'd ever seen in her life. She knew there was no way she'd have the strength to tell her, but it was that thought that had her blue eyes sparkling.

"Hi there," Shenin said, smiling down at her.

"You… again?" Tyler asked, blinking slowly as unconsciousness tried desperately to reclaim her.

"Oh, look who's got her sense of humor back," Shenin said, smiling brightly. Reaching out, she placed her hand on Tyler's head, palm side down, her thumb brushed back and forth over her friends forehead soothingly. "That'll help you with this battle you need to fight right now," she said, tears coming to her eyes again, "I need you to come through this, okay? You need to use every bit of that strength you have to get better, okay? Please?"

Tyler was using that strength to stay conscious at that point. "I'll… try," she said, before a cough over took her and left her breathless.

Shenin nodded, pressing her lips together so she wouldn't completely lose it. "You need to know," she said, "that I called your parents." Tyler's expression quickly changed. "Don't worry," Shenin told her, touching her hand, "I told them that you were going to be fine, that you were hurt saving someone in your unit, and that you were fighting your way back. So you need to not prove me to be a liar, you understand?" That was almost an order.

"Yes… ma'am," Tyler said, overwhelmed by emotion at that point. Shenin had taken into account her father's bad heart, and had eased the shock of their daughter being hurt. That knowledge and the gratitude that seemed to engulf her suddenly was more than Tyler could handle at that point.

Reaching up Tyler grasped Shenin's hand in hers, her look displaying her appreciation, "Just... in... case," she began.

"No!" Shenin said, wrenching her hand away. "You will not say your goodbyes, Tyler, you will not!" Tears were in her eyes at that point, and with a blink they were streaming down her face.

Tyler closed her eyes slowly, tears leaking out of hers as well.

"Shen..." She began again, shaking her head.

"Don't do it, Tyler," Shenin said.

"Devereaux!" came a yell from the doorway. "Transport is wheels up in five, get your ass out there!"

Shenin flinched, then leaned down, her face next to Tyler's, "You better fight for me," she said, in a whisper. "I love you more than life itself, and I will not lose you." With that she kissed Tyler's lips softly. Then she pivoted on her heel and left the room.

"She does make an exit, doesn't she?" Sheila said, smiling.

Tyler closed her eyes, smiling despite the overwhelming feeling of sadness weighing on her. Fortunately, she was unconscious again a few minutes later.

Shenin traveled back to Alaska, her mind still on Tyler. When she got into Eielson, she went straight to her captain's office.

She knocked on his door and heard him bark, "Come!"

Stepping into the office, she snapped to attention instantly, and saluted.

Chappy looked at her, his grey eyes narrowed.

"Did you have a nice vacation?" he asked, not returning her salute.

"No sir," she replied, her eyes staring straight ahead.

"Well, that's a damned shame, because you're going on report for this, and you're damned lucky I didn't list you as AWOL!" he snarled.

"Yes, sir, thank you, sir," she replied, feeling her vision starting to blur because she was so tired. She was on duty in a half an hour and she didn't even have time to eat or shower.

"Is that all you have to say for yourself?" he asked, his face a mask of stone.

"I have no excuse, sir," Shenin replied, closing her eyes for a moment to try and clear them.

"What is your problem, lieutenant?" Chappy asked, having noticed her stance wavering.

"I'm sorry, sir…" Shenin began, but that's when she blacked out.

Chappy had to lunge forward to catch her before she hit the ground; she was out cold.

"Anne!"

She ran in, responding to the panic in his voice.

"Oh, my god, what happened?!" she cried, moving to Shenin's face.

"I don't know," Chappy said, moving to pick Shenin up to take her over to the couch, "she just passed out."

Anne gave her boss a stern look. "You were yelling at her," she said, her tone disapproving.

"Careful, airman," he growled.

"Sir, she's been on a plane for over a day, and it doesn't look like she's slept the entire time. Her best friend was injured in Iraq, an IED blew up in front of her, and she saved another airman, but got caught by it herself. Lieutenant Devereaux traveled to see if her friend was dead or not."

It was more than Anne had ever said to him at one time, and while she was his assistant, she never defended anyone that didn't deserve defending. Captain Chapman found himself feeling bad about his treatment of the young woman lying on his couch.

"She didn't tell me any of that," he told Anne.

"She wouldn't, sir," Anne said, getting up to get water out of his fridge and using it to dampen a napkin. She applied it to Shenin's forehead. "Lieutenant?" she queried, blotting Shenin's face with the napkin.

Shenin began to stir. Opening her eyes she looked disoriented.

"You with us Devereaux?" Chappy said, his voice gruff.

"I'm…" Shenin began, "yes, yes, sir," she said, moving to try and get up.

"No, no, no," Anne said, putting her hands on Shenin's shoulders to keep her down, and giving her boss a stern look. "You passed out, lieutenant, just lay still for a minute."

Shenin nodded wearily, lying back. After ten minutes she was finally feeling strong enough to get up. Glancing at her watch, she said, "I need to get to my squad room."

"You go home," Chappy said, "Get some sleep, get something to eat, we'll see you tomorrow."

Shenin blinked a couple of times, looking at Anne, who winked at her.

"I'll make sure she gets home," Anne said. "If that's okay with you sir?"

"Go, go," he said, wanting the whole scene to be over.

Minutes later they were in Anne's car driving towards officers' quarters.

"How is she?" Anne asked, concerned.

"Alive," Shenin said, still feeling exhausted.

"But?" Anne asked, knowing there was more, Shenin looked so devastated it was unfathomable.

"She's in critical condition, and they're not sure she's going to make it," Shenin said, saying it quickly so she didn't have to relive it again.

"Oh, my God..." Anne said, unable to believe what she was hearing. She had tears in her eyes as she pulled up in front of the officers' quarters.

"I have to go," Shenin said, reaching blindly for the door handle as the tears started again.

"Shenin!" Anne called, but Shenin was shaking her head.

"I can't... I just...please..." Shenin said, climbing out of the car and running inside.

Fortunately, she found her keys quickly and got into her apartment. Closing the door behind her, she crumpled to the floor, crying uncontrollably. Eventually she picked herself up off the floor and dragged herself into her room, where she laid on the bed and cried herself into an exhausted sleep.

The next morning she woke, and with steely resolve she got out of bed, and took a shower. Forcing her mind away from any thoughts of Tyler, she moved as if in a trance, putting on her uniform, tying her boots, pulling her hair up and securing it.

The entire unit noticed that she not only looked exhausted, but extremely haunted. They also noticed that the captain's assistant spent the entire day shadowing them.

In the end it was Anne that got Shenin through the next few weeks. She picked her up and took her to work, and brought her home again. She stayed with her at night to make sure she ate, and then tucked her into bed. They didn't talk much, Shenin just couldn't talk about Tyler until she heard how she was. Sheila was sending updates, but unfortunately there wasn't a lot to tell.

It was a full month before Sheila wrote to say, "Tyler is finally out of the woods. She's resting after the last of the surgeries. Still really weak."

It was another two weeks later when Shenin's phone rang at six am.

She answered it, thinking it might be Sheila.

"What're you doin'?" came the most wonderful voice she'd ever heard in her life.

"Tyler," she breathed, so happy she could barely think.

"Hi babe," Tyler said, sounding out of breath herself, but for a whole other reason, like a healing collapsed lung.

"Oh my God it is so good to hear your voice," Shenin said, tears in her eyes.

"Don't you start crying," Tyler said, her voice softening.

"I'm sorry," Shenin said, wiping at her tears, "so how are you?"

"Still feel like Hell," Tyler said, her voice strained and a bit out of breath.

"Almost getting blown up will do that to a person," Shenin said, conversationally.

"You don't say," Tyler said, grinning on her end.

"Yeah, I do," Shenin said, "and you damned well better not ever do anything like that again."

"Definitely not on my list of repeats," Tyler said.

"I was so scared, Ty," Shenin said, her voice reflecting that fear.

"I know," Tyler said, her voice sad. "I'm so sorry I put you through that."

"You saved Jean's life, Ty, it's not like I'm blaming you for doing that, please don't think that's what I'm doing. I understand why you did what you did, it's who you are. I'm just really glad you didn't end up paying for that with your life."

Tyler was quiet for a few moments, letting Shenin's voice wash over her. It felt so good just to hear her voice again, to feel all the feelings that talking to her created inside her head and her heart.

"Ty?" Shenin queried.

"I'm here," Tyler said, her voice gravelly.

"You sound so tired," Shenin said.

"Yeah, I am, that shit they give you for surgeries is killer."

"Get some rest, Ty, it'll help you recover faster," Shenin said, loathe to let Tyler off the phone, but knowing that she needed to rest.

Tyler made a noise indicating that she didn't want to get off the phone.

"It's okay, babe," Shenin said. "I'll be right here on the other end of the phone whenever you want to call. No matter what time it is, okay?"

"Okay," Tyler said, her tone petulant, so much so that it made Shenin smile.

"Okay," Shenin said nodding, "get some rest."

"Hey," Tyler said, forestalling Shenin saying goodbye.

"What?" Shenin asked softly.

"I love you," Tyler said so softly that Shenin had tears in her eyes instantly.

"Oh, Ty…" she said, her tears in her voice. "I love you. Thank you for getting better."

"Anything for you," Tyler replied. "I will call you again soon, okay?"

"Okay," Shenin said, feeling beyond happy. "Good night."

"Good morning," Tyler replied, grinning.

Leaving her apartment that morning, Shenin couldn't believe how happy she was. Tyler was okay, and she loved her. She'd finally said it, said it the right way. *Oh my God!* was all Shenin's mind could think over and over again. She avoided thinking about the rest, and how impossible it would be, and that Tyler still had her issues with all of this. No, she wasn't going to think about that right now, she was going to enjoy this feeling, damnit!

There were a few hitches in Tyler's recovery, a couple of infections that needed to be treated with antibiotics, which slowed her recovery. By early September, she seemed to be doing better again. The doctors were still watching her closely, concerned about her lung healing, not sure if they were happy with her progress. She was still consistently out of breath and it was decided on September 19 that they needed to go back in to see what was happening with her lung. Tyler was not happy.

"If they think it's necessary, Ty, you need to let them do it," Shenin reasoned.

"I just want my fucking life back," Tyler growled, started to cough as she did.

"See? That's not good, babe," she said. "You're still coughing so much, and you keep getting short of breath. You can't get your strength back if you can't breathe."

"I know," Tyler said, hating this more than anything, it was just another setback.

"It'll be okay, Ty," Shenin said, she was feeling a little bit helpless, being so far away.

"I know, babe, I know," Tyler said, "I'm doing it."

"Thank you," Shenin said.

"You're welcome," Tyler said.

"You should get some rest," Shenin said, hearing that Tyler was getting tired again.

"Okay," Tyler said, giving in easily because she was getting really tired. "I love you," she said, her voice just as soft as it had been the very first time she'd told Shenin that.

"I love you," Shenin said, with equal intensity.

The day after Tyler's surgery, there was a sudden flurry of activity on the base in Alaska. Shenin and her unit were out on the front line, patrolling when they heard a lot of people whooping and hollering. Gina's phone rang, and she looked at Shenin apologetically.

"Get it," Shenin said. "It might be someone telling us what's going on."

Gina answered the phone and listened intently. Her eyes grew wide, filling with tears and she looked over at Shenin. When she hung up the phone, she looked almost faint.

"What is it?" Shenin asked, worried.

"They just announced it," Gina said, looking shell-shocked, shaking her head, as if denying what she was saying as she said it. "They've taken down Don't Ask, Don't Tell."

Shenin's mouth dropped open in complete shock. "Oh my God..." Shenin said, tears coming to her eyes.

"It's about fucking time," said one of the guys in the unit.

"Got that right!" yelled someone else.

Gina and Shenin looked at each other, smiling through their tears.

It was a weekend of celebration at almost every Air Force base in the country and the world. Gays that had been hiding for years could suddenly breathe. It was amazing!

"Gay pipe-dream, huh?" Shenin said, smiling as she held the phone close to her ear.

"Guess it was a pretty good pipe," Tyler said, tiredly. She'd been out of surgery for eighteen hours, but was still feeling the effects of the anesthesia.

"It is such wonderful news," Shenin said, smiling from ear to ear.

"It is," Tyler agreed.

"I'm sorry, babe, I know you're still in a fog, I'll let you rest," Shenin said. "I just had to make sure you'd heard."

"Couldn't miss it around here," Tyler said, smiling.

"Good," Shenin said, "okay, go to sleep, Tyler."

Tyler made that petulant sound in the back of her throat.

"Stop it," Shenin said, grinning, "you need your rest."

Tyler sighed, "I know," she said, still petulant, "I love you," she said then.

"I love you," Shenin replied.

They hung up then.

CHAPTER 9

The next month was spent with few calls from Tyler as she was busy trying to get well enough to get out of the hospital at some time in the future.

One afternoon, Shenin and her squad were out on the flight line doing drills, and working on maneuvers. They were making their way across the flight line, when Shenin got a call from control telling her to clear the flight line and that a transport was landing. Shenin and her unit double-timed it to the far end of the line; they were standing talking amongst themselves when the transport landed.

Anne walked up at that point, handing Shenin a report from Captain Chapman. Shenin was reading the report as the people started disembarking from the plane. The rumble of a large vehicle starting up and backing out of the transport caused Shenin to glance up and scan the group getting off the plane. They were far enough away, and it was bright enough that Shenin needed to shade her eyes and squint, but one person had a very distinct gait, that seemed familiar. She continued to stare; the woman was in civilian clothes and just then the wind picked up slightly and that's when Shenin saw the curls.

"Tyler?" she said, a look of shock on her face. "Tyler!" she practically screamed as she saw the black cowboy boots. She took off at a dead run, closing the distance between them quickly. As everyone looked on, Shenin launched herself at Tyler, who simply opened her arms and scooped the smaller woman up.

"Oh my god, oh my god," Shenin said over and over again, tears running down her face. "You're here, you're here... oh my god, Tyler..." she said, burying her face in Tyler's neck, desperately praying this wasn't a dream.

"I'm here, babe," Tyler said, stroking her hair and holding on to her tightly. "It's okay, I'm here, I got you..."

When Shenin finally leaned back, and looked up into Tyler's face, her eyes were so golden, Tyler was sure she'd melt right into them. Leaning in, she touched her lips to Shenin's and Shenin immediately wrapped her arms around Tyler's neck, pressing her body closer, and giving in to the longest, deepest kiss of her life. It was pure heaven, and Shenin didn't care who saw. It took her a full minute before she heard the whoops and hollering going on from her unit. She and Tyler broke into a laugh.

Pulling back, Shenin gazed at Tyler. "You're here, how are you here?" she asked, still out of breath from the kiss.

"I had to see my girl..." Tyler said, smiling.

"But why didn't you tell me you were coming?" Shenin asked, having just talked to her the day before.

"I wanted to surprise you," Tyler told her simply.

"Well, you managed it," Shenin said, grinning.

They were walking across the flight line, arm in arm. Anne walked over, leaning up to hug Tyler. "Good to see you looking well," Anne said, smiling.

"It's good to be seen, looking well," Tyler said, smiling.

"Ty," Shenin said, gesturing to the side where her unit was standing watching, "this is my unit. Adams, Green, Sanchez," she said, pointing to each man in turn, Tyler extended her hand to each of them in turn. "Aims, Beech, and Cannel," Tyler shook hands with each of the other members, lingering longest on Cannel, her eyes connecting with the younger woman's a moment longer than necessary. Gina's eyes narrowed slightly and she nodded, as if she'd just gotten a subliminal message, which she had. That message was, *I'm here now, and that's my girl, so hands off.*

"Everyone, this is Senior Airman Tyler Hancock, and she just got back from Iraq after being wounded in combat, where she saved another airman's life."

"Yeah!" Aims said, pumping his fist as everyone else clapped and whistled.

Tyler looked over at Shenin, a wry grin on her face, "Always making me out to be the hero."

"Pardon me, ma'am," Green said, his tone respectful, "but if you saved another airman's life, you are very definitely a hero."

Tyler looked back at the man for a long moment, then inclined her head, then nodded.

Shenin put her hand in Tyler's squeezing it. "Now, everyone is done for the day, 'cause I'm gonna take my hero home."

With that they walked hand in hand to the parking lot, and Shenin took Tyler over to her car, opening her trunk so Tyler could put her duffle in.

Tyler gave a low whistle, running her hand along the rear fender. "Just beautiful," she said, smiling.

"Wait till you hear it start," Shenin said, grinning.

"Go for it," Tyler said, standing back.

Shenin got in, turned the key and the car started with a deep rumble. Tyler got in on the passenger side, and looked over at her. "Almost as good as sex," she said, leaning over to pull Shenin to her again, kissing her deeply.

When they parted they were both breathless. "I still can't believe you're here," Shenin said, her awed tone backing up that statement.

"I'm here babe," Tyler said, here blue eyes staring down into Shenin's.

Reaching up, Shenin touched Tyler's cheek. "You look so tired, Ty," Shenin said. "You're still not a hundred percent are you?"

Tyler shook her head. "No, not yet, and that ridiculously long flight didn't really help."

"I know, it sucks, doesn't it?" Shenin said. "Okay, so you just sit back and relax and I'll get you to my place, and then you can get some rest, okay?

Tyler leaned back against the leather seat, closing her eyes and nodding. Shenin put the car into gear and gunned the engine. Tyler looked around a few minutes later and realized they were off the base.

"I thought you lived on base," Tyler said.

"I did, I moved about two weeks ago to a house off base."

"Oh," Tyler replied, nodding. "Okay."

They made it to Shenin's house in twenty minutes. It was a nice two story in a town called Moose Creek, just north of the base. Tyler was asleep when they pulled up. Shenin glanced over at her a number of times during the drive, still unable to believe she was there.

Shutting off the car, Shenin reached over touching Tyler's hand. "Ty?" she said, softly.

Tyler opened her eyes, looking around herself. "We're here?"

"Yeah, we're here," Shenin said, smiling. "Come on."

They got out of the car, and Shenin popped the trunk, reaching in to pick up Tyler's duffle.

"I got it," Tyler said, moving to take it from her.

"No," Shenin said, "I got it, just head to the front door." When Tyler hesitated, Shenin narrowed her eyes. "March, airman!" she ordered.

Tyler grinned. "So bossy now that she's an LT," she muttered.

Shenin laughed. "That's right."

Once they were inside, Shenin set Tyler's duffel down in the entryway. Turning she took Tyler's hand and lead her upstairs taking her straight to her bedroom. As Tyler looked on with a bemused look on her face, Shenin reached up and took off the Harley Davidson jacket Tyler was wearing, laying it aside. She pushed Tyler to a sitting position on the bed, and knelt down to pull off her cowboy boots. Then she pushed Tyler back on the bed, so her head rested on the pillows piled at the head of the bed.

"Now," Shenin said, giving Tyler a stern look, "you lay there and sleep for a bit, I'll wake you up when dinner is ready, okay?"

Tyler reached up, touching Shenin on the cheek, sliding her hand to her temple, her blue eyes looking both tired and wistful.

"Are you taking care of me?" Tyler asked.

Shenin smiled fondly. "I guess I am," she said.

Tyler slid her hand around to the back of Shenin's head, pulling her down to kiss her lips softly and then pulling her down to lie next to her on the bed. Shenin rested her head in the hollow of Tyler's shoulder, breathing in the scent of the woman who'd been a constant thought for so long now. She felt Tyler's hand at the small of her back, and her other hand stroking her hair. They lay together for a long time, eventually Shenin felt Tyler's breath become even, and she knew she was asleep again. Glancing up, she confirmed this. Staring up at Tyler, her eyes took in the strong jaw line, the smooth skin, the light eyelashes, then her eyes rested on the tiny still-healing scar on her cheek from the IED. Taking a slow deep breath, she reminded herself that Tyler was here now, and she was okay, that was what mattered the most.

Carefully getting off the bed, Shenin picked up Tyler's jacket and boots and took them to her closet to set them inside. Walking out of her closet she looked again at the woman lying on her bed. Tyler's legs were crossed at the ankles and one hand rested on her chest now, the other arm she'd thrown up over her head. Shenin found that she couldn't help but look at her, so slim, yet strong, and so very attractive, her long flowing curls spread out on the pillow around her.

Shenin sighed, she knew it was probably dangerous to love someone this much, but she didn't care. It felt so good to have her here. She didn't know how long it would be for, or what the future held. What she did know was that she loved this woman to distraction, and she was going to take whatever she could get at this point.

Three hours later, Shenin walked into the room, Tyler had turned over on her side by that time. Sitting down next to her on the bed, Shenin reached down, touching Tyler's cheek.

"Ty..." she said, softly.

"Hmm?" Tyler murmured stirring and opening her eyes. Shenin knew she would never get over how very blue Tyler's eyes were. "Hi..." Tyler said, smiling tiredly.

"Hi," Shenin said, smiling down at her. "Are you hungry?" she asked, "or would you rather sleep some more?"

Tyler closed her eyes for a moment and then opened them. "Kind of starving," she said, grinning, "you know the dinner service on the plane was, well, non-existent."

Shenin laughed, as she moved to stand up and take Tyler's hand to help her up. "I know, I took one of those flights, the service sucks!"

Tyler stood, grabbing her by the waist and pulling her close, her arms encircling her waist. "I know you did," she said, her eyes staring down into Shenin's, "twice in less than a week," she continued, her tone very affected. "You'll never know how much it meant to me that you were there," she said, shaking her head, her look awed. "You were the one thing I needed to see when I woke up from that nightmare that first time, and you were there."

"I had to be there, Ty," Shenin said, her eyes scanning Tyler's face. "I needed to see you, to be there, to know you were okay."

"But I wasn't okay," Tyler said, "and I have to tell you," she said, putting her lips right next to Shenin's ear, "that last thing you said to me was what made me fight my ass off to get better."

Shenin swallowed hard, trying to hold back the tears that were once again threatening to overwhelm her. Tyler recognized the movement, and pulled her close. That was when Shenin lost all composure and cried. Tyler ended up sitting back down on the bed, pulling Shenin down onto her lap, holding her cradled on her lap while Shenin cried. It broke her heart that she'd put this woman through so much, but it also touched her heart that she meant this much to someone, it was an astounding feeling.

When Shenin had calmed down, Tyler tipped her chin up to look at her, her thumb wiping away the tears. "Feel better?" she asked, feeling a tug on her heart at seeing Shenin's red- rimmed eyes.

Shenin sniffled. “No,” she said, “crying always makes me feel worse.”

“Then stop doing it,” Tyler said, grinning.

“Brat,” Shenin said, grinning now too.

“Uh-huh,” Tyler said, smiling.

“Come on, your dinner is getting cold.”

They had dinner, and Tyler noted that it was one of her favorites.

“Did you go shopping?” Tyler asked.

“When?” Shenin asked.

“Earlier,” Tyler asked.

“Uh, no, why?”

“You just happened to have all of this to make me dinner? And it just happened to be one of my favorites?” Tyler asked, trying to work it out in her head.

“I have it, because it’s your favorite,” Shenin said. “And now it’s one of my favorites too.”

Tyler shook her head, wondering if there was ever going to be an end to the things this woman could say to make her feel special. She was seriously beginning to doubt it.

After dinner, Tyler went to take a shower and Shenin sat on her bed, reading reports. She looked up as Tyler walked out of the bathroom, noting that she wore her Air Force sweats, and a t-shirt.

"Feel better?" Shenin asked, as Tyler moved to lay face down on the bed next to her.

"Much," Tyler said, her voice muffled because it was against the comforter.

Tyler turned over, lying on her back and looking up at Shenin.

"Do you have a lot of work to do tonight?" she asked.

"No," Shenin said, immediately setting the reports aside and moving to lie down on her side, resting her head on her hand, "I was just killing time until you were done."

Tyler grinned. "I know you have to work, Shen, I didn't expect you to drop everything when I showed up."

"I don't have to work tonight, Tyler, and that's that," Shenin replied.

"Yes, ma'am…" Tyler said, grinning.

Shenin placed her free hand on Tyler's chest, tracing a line down to her arm, there she saw the edge of a red-ish scar. She looked up at Tyler and saw that Tyler was watching her closely.

"When am I going to see it?" Tyler asked, referring to the damage that had been caused by the IED. She knew it was why was wearing a t-shirt instead of her customary tank top for bed.

Tyler closed her eyes for a moment, then looked back at Shenin. "Not yet, okay?" she asked, her tone soft. "I can't even stand to look at it yet," she added.

Shenin nodded, her eyes dropping from Tyler's.

"Hey," Tyler said, "I will let you see it, okay? I just… not yet, okay?"

"Okay," Shenin said, feeling sad that this was obviously such a hard thing for Tyler, but understanding it too. She'd been loath to wear anything sleeveless for a long time after she'd been shot in the shoulder, she could only imagine what kind of damage the IED had done to Tyler's body.

"So," Shenin said after a long moment, wanting to shift the conversation, "how long do I have you for?" she asked.

Tyler looked up at her, an odd look in her eyes that Shenin didn't understand.

"Well, that kind of depends," Tyler said.

"On?" Shenin asked.

"Well, the Air Force has kindly given me some time to recover from my injuries, and I was thinking that it would be better to rest and recover in Alaska… but I'd need a place to stay…"

"Not funny, Tyler," Shenin said, narrowing her eyes dangerously.

"Okay, okay," Tyler said, grinning. "I didn't want to assume anything."

"Uh-huh," Shenin said, still giving Tyler a vile look. "So how long will I have a house guest?" She asked, trying not to sound overly hopefully.

That's when Tyler's look changed. "Well, I have to report to OTS on December fourth, so…"

"What!?" Shenin cried, clearly shocked. "You got into OTS? And you didn't tell me!?" That had her giving Tyler's arm a shove playfully.

Tyler laughed, coughing at the same time. "This was part of that surprise thing," she pointed out.

"No kidding," Shenin said, shaking her head, then she looked back at Tyler. "I'm so proud of you, Ty, that is amazing news."

Tyler nodded. "I figured it was the least I could do for you," she said.

"For me?" Shenin queried.

"Originally to eliminate the issue with fraternization, the pres was kind enough to get rid of DADT for me after that," she said, grinning.

"Nice guy," Shenin agreed, "so, that means I've got you here for just over a month?"

Tyler nodded. "I need to get back into shape, or OTS is gonna kill me."

"I can help with that," Shenin said, smiling.

"Can you now?" Tyler said, grinning mischievously. "Hey, speaking of getting into shape," Tyler said, her tone changing with her raised eyebrow. "Wasn't I supposed to get a video of that cardio dance thing you were doing?"

"Yes," Shenin said, "but then you went and got all serious on me and managed to get yourself blown up, so..."

"So all bets are off then?" Tyler finished for her.

"No," Shenin said, "But, since you're here, maybe you can go with me to a class."

"Me, in a cardio dance class?" Tyler asked, looking skeptical.

Shenin gave her a narrowed look. "You could do it," she said, her tone sure.

"I doubt that, but I know I couldn't at this point," Tyler said. "So, wait, you said you could help me, you didn't mean the cardio dance thing, right? Or did you mean…" she asked, her grin wry as her face took on a suggestive look.

"That is not what I meant!" Shenin said, laughing.

"Damn!" Tyler said, laughing too.

"Well, I didn't mean that I can't help out there too…" Shenin said, her voice trailing off as she leaned down, kissing Tyler's lips.

Tyler's hand reached up to cup the back of her head, pulling her closer. They kissed passionately for a few minutes, things were heating up when Tyler pulled back, breathing heavily.

"Shen, wait," she said, holding up a hand.

"What is it?" Shenin asked, thinking that Tyler was changing her mind about them again.

Tyler saw the look in her eyes. "No, babe," she said, shaking her head, "you have no idea how much I want to do this right now, I mean, seriously, but…" She breathed, closing her eyes momentarily, then opening them again and looking up into Shenin's eyes. "But I want the first time we're together this way to be perfect, and I'm not really up to that right now…" she said, her voice trailing off as she dropped her head, then peaked up with one eye, "do you understand?"

Shenin smiled softly. "Yes, I understand," she said, "I can wait. Hell, I've waited this long, right?"

"You better have," Tyler countered.

"Speaking of which," Shenin said, narrowing her eyes.

"Uh-oh," Tyler said, sensing she was about to catch hell for something.

"I caught that little exchange today between you and Cannel," Shenin said.

Tyler pressed her tongue against her teeth, making a sound Shenin took to mean Tyler had no intention to apologize for it. She canted her head to the side waiting for Tyler to say something.

Tyler shrugged. "I needed to make sure she understood."

"Understood what?" Shenin asked.

"That you belong to me," Tyler said simply, but with enough intensity in her eyes to make Shenin realize she was very serious.

"Tyler," Shenin said, her tone exasperated, "she was no threat to you, she never was."

Tyler smiled wisely. "Yeah, well, now there's no question. Which reminds me," she said, then her tone deepening slightly, "before I leave here, we will be going back to that bar Anne took you to."

"For?" Shenin asked.

"So every bitch in there knows who you belong to," Tyler said, her tone deadly serious.

"I do, huh?" Shenin asked, her tone playful in spite of Tyler's tone.

Tyler narrowed her blue eyes at her. "You will most certainly belong to me by then."

Shenin felt her breath catch in her throat, the sexual innuendo was so strong, she felt a pull deep inside her in reaction to it.

"Oh my God," Shenin breathed.

"What?" Tyler asked, her tone still deep.

"I just met the rock star," Shenin said, grinning, her eyes sparkling.

Tyler rolled her eyes, clearing her throat distinctly, "That stuff?"

"I think Anne's right about you," Shenin said. "I just think you don't know it, you're just being you. But the you, that you are, is so damned attractive that no woman who catches you wants to ever let you go."

"Uh-huh," Tyler said, sounding unconvinced.

"You don't have to believe it, Ty," Shenin said, "for it to be true. As for me," she said then, "I belong to you, I have since the day we met. No one is ever going to mean to me what you mean, ever."

Tyler leaned in kissing her again, then leaned back, looking at her.

"I need you to promise me something," Tyler said, her tone serious.

"Okay," Shenin said, "what?"

"If we're really going to do this, us," she clarified, gesturing between them.

"If?" Shenin countered, her look darkening.

"Okay, okay," Tyler said, holding up her hand defensively. "I just meant that I'm finally ready to do this with you, but for me to be totally committed, I need one promise from you."

"What do you need me to promise, Ty?"

"That if at any point in time throughout this; the next month; the next six months; the next year; whatever, if you decide you can't do this, it's not for you or it's not what you thought, I want you to promise that you'll just be honest with me. Can you do that?"

"Tyler…" Shenin began, her tone edging on exasperated.

"No," Tyler said shaking her head. "Don't tell me it couldn't happen, because I'm here to tell you it can. What we're doing here, you and me, is just asking for trouble. We don't know what's going to happen when I get done with OTS, we don't know where they're going to send me, I could end up back in fucking Iraq for all I know. That's not going to be easy on either of us. Time, distance, being away from each other for so long is going to take its toll on this relationship, and we'd be stupid not to see that." Again she had to hold her hand up to stop what Shenin was going to say. "Please don't say anything yet, I need you to understand. You are not just some chick I want to date, okay? This is going to be huge, and if it doesn't work, I know for sure it's going to a rip a hole in my soul. So I need to know that you're willing to see reality for what it is and that you will at least put us both out of our misery if it comes to that."

Shenin stared back at Tyler for what seemed like hours, finally blowing her breath out miserably. "Okay, I promise," she said, her tone rushed.

"Shen…" Tyler began, but it was Shenin's turn to hold up her hand to forestall her.

"I understand, Tyler," she practically snapped, "I do. Okay?"

Tyler looked back at her, and Shenin could literally see her taking a mental step back.

"I'm sorry," Shenin said, closing her eyes so she wouldn't have to see the look in Tyler's for a moment, "I just…" she began, hesitating, trying to think of the right words to use, "I hate that you're thinking of the end, before we've even started."

Tyler looked back at her for a long moment, and Shenin could see she was going over in her mind what Shenin had just said. Finally, she blew her breath out in a sigh, dropping her head for a long moment.

When she looked up at Shenin again, her blue eyes had tears in them. "I'm scared to death," she said simply.

"Why?" Shenin asked.

Tyler sighed, shaking her head. "Because I want this so much, and I'm terrified that I'm getting it, and that something is going to happen, and I just can't—"

Shenin's lips on hers stopped her, Shenin's hands in her hair, caressing, stroking, grasping as they kissed her mind stilled. She felt Shenin's lips move from hers to her cheek and then to her ear.

"Let's just live this, and enjoy this and stop worrying about the future for a bit, okay?"

Tyler couldn't argue with that, so she didn't. Turning on her side to face Shenin, she pulled her into her arms, hugging her close. Pulling back, she looked down at Shenin, her blue eyes warm.

"I love you," Tyler said, her voice soft and sweet.

"So that's what that looks like," Shenin said, smiling.

"What?" Tyler asked.

"When you tell me you love me, that's how your face looks," Shenin said, touching Tyler's cheek, looking right into her eyes. "I love you," she said.

"Yeah…" Tyler said, smiling now too, "that looks pretty good."

Tyler pulled Shenin back into her arms; they lay that way until they both fell asleep.

The next day, Shenin had to go in because she had things scheduled with her team, so Tyler took the opportunity to have lunch with Anne and catch up. Shenin had Tyler drop her off at the squad room, and let her take the car to pick up Anne.

"You sure you trust me with this beautiful car?" Tyler asked, grinning.

"I trust you with my life, Ty," Shenin said, smiling. "Cars can be replaced."

With that she got out of the car. They'd decided they should be more careful on base with their affection, since Tyler was technically still enlisted and Shenin was an officer. The fraternization rule was still in place, even if Don't Ask, Don't Tell had been abolished.

Tyler drove to pick up Anne at the captain's office. She was waiting outside.

"She let you use her car, huh?" Anne asked, as she got in on the passenger side.

"Well, it was either this, or her Shadow, and I thought it might be a little too chilly for that." Tyler said, grinning.

"Right!" Anne said, laughing.

Tyler headed back to the front gates of the base, and then Anne gave her directions from there.

Anne looked over at Tyler as she drove. "So you're really okay?" she asked.

Tyler glanced over at Anne, seeing the concern on her face, nodding, she said, "Yeah, I'm okay. I'm still doing some recovery, but they said I'll be fine."

"Good," Anne said, nodding her head. "I gotta tell ya Tyler, that whole thing really spun Shenin."

Tyler nodded, her look serious. "I understand, though," she said, then, "that I have you to thank for getting her through that."

Anne smiled. "Well, I was just trying to help," she said humbly, "I really like her, she's a very genuine person, that's rare."

"Yeah, she's definitely one of a kind," Tyler said, smiling fondly.

"And man does she love you," Anne said, sounding awed. "You have got to know that, Tyler, there shouldn't ever be a doubt in your mind how much that woman loves you. When she got back here from Iraq she collapsed from being so tired, in the captain's office no less! When I could get anything out of her, she couldn't even remember the last time she'd eaten something. She was a mess, and she worried about you constantly."

Tyler pressed her lips together, Shenin hadn't told her any of this, but then again, Shenin wasn't one to play up hurts and problems. She was no drama queen that was for sure.

"Well, have no doubt," Tyler told Anne, "I love her with every fiber of my being, I'm just praying we can make it as a couple."

"Why wouldn't you?" Anne asked, dismayed.

"I'm headed to OTS in December," Tyler said.

"So request Alaska as a post," Anne said.

"Right and they'll just give it to me 'cause I'm cute," Tyler said sarcastically.

"Well, you could take her back East and marry her," Anne said glibly.

"Jesus, can we at least have sex first?" Tyler laughed.

"Oh," Anne said, shocked, "you two haven't…"

"No," Tyler said, already regretting saying what she did.

"Who are you and what have you done with Tyler Hancock?" Anne asked.

"Stop it," Tyler said, grinning in spite of herself.

"You're not usually one to waste time, Tyler."

"Yeah, well I'm not usually recovering from almost having my head blown off by an IED either."

"Oh, yeah, true," Anne said, nodding, "All I'm saying is that maybe after all this shit, fate will see fit to put you two together on the same base."

"Fate's not always my friend," Tyler said, her tone bland.

Later at the restaurant, Tyler and Anne were talking, when Anne glanced over Tyler's shoulder. "Uh..." Anne said, grinning, "someone is giving you the eye."

"Oh for God's sake," Tyler said, shaking her head as she glanced behind, catching the eye of a blond sitting at the next table. The girl smiled at her, Tyler inclined her head, and then looked back at Anne. Anne was grinning widely.

"Shut up," Tyler said simply.

A little while later, the blond went past the table, and headed to the bathroom. Anne watched her go, looking back at Tyler. Tyler was in love, but she wasn't blind, the blond was hot. When she saw Anne looking at her, she narrowed her eyes. "Shut up," she said again.

When the blond came back by, she looked at Tyler hard. Her eyes dropped from Tyler's face, and looked at the shirt she wore. Tyler was wearing an Air force shirt, her Harley Davidson jacket was slung over her chair. She was also wearing her customary jeans and cowboy boots.

Smiling intensely, the girl stopped in front of Tyler. "Hi," she said, looking Tyler right in the eyes.

"Hi," Tyler said, smiling, and trying to ignore the look that Anne was giving her from across the table.

"You're Air Force?" The girl asked.

Tyler nodded.

"I'm Candy," the girl said, extending her hand to Tyler.

"Tyler," Tyler said, "and that's Anne," she said, nodding to her friend.

"Hi," Candy said, barely sparing Anne a glance, which had Anne grinning wider. "So, I just want to say that I think what you airmen do is amazing, and I really want to thank you for all you do for our country."

Tyler did her best to subdue her grin. "Well, thank you Candy," she said, trying to get the conversation over with quickly.

"Are you stationed here at Eielson?" Candy asked.

"Uh, no," Tyler said, "I'm stationed at Nellis."

"That's in Vegas, right?" Candy asked.

"Yeah," Tyler said, nodding.

"But she just came back from Iraq," Anne put in, giving Tyler a raised eyebrow; Tyler could have killed her.

"Oh, my God, really? That's crazy! Did you see any action over there?" Candy asked, the look in her eyes indicating the double entendre.

Before Tyler could open her mouth Anne put in. "She almost got killed by an IED."

"Anne," Tyler said, giving her a, *what the fuck are you doing?* look. "Candy doesn't want to hear about that."

"Of course, I do, you're a wounded soldier," Candy said.

"I'm also a very taken soldier," Tyler said, her tone as nice as she could make it.

"Oh," Candy said, looking disappointed, but getting the hint. "Lucky girl…" she said and then walked away, staring at Tyler over her shoulder.

"Jesus," Tyler said, shaking her, head, then giving Anne a dirty look, "are you crazy?"

Anne started to laugh. "No, I just love to see the way they get all excited," she said, grinning. "You still attract them like there's no tomorrow."

"S'okay," Tyler said, grinning, "I'm going to tell Shenin what you just did, and I'm going to let her kick your ass for it."

"That's not cool," Anne said, laughing.

Later that night, Tyler and Shenin were lying in bed watching TV after having dinner. Tyler was sitting with her back against the headboard, and Shenin was lying with her head against Tyler's abdomen.

"She did what?" Shenin asked, glancing up at Tyler.

"Told this complete stranger that I'd almost been killed by an IED," Tyler said, shaking her head.

Shenin grinned. "She was testing your rock star status," she said.

"Yeah, by hanging me out as bait to this chick, that doesn't bug you?" Tyler asked.

Shenin looked up at her. "Did you take this chick up on anything?" she asked.

"No," Tyler said.

"Then why should it bug me?" Shenin asked. "It just reconfirms that I'm dating a very hot woman, who is much desired by other women."

Tyler shook her head, looking down at her.

"What?" Shenin asked.

"You're nothing like anyone I've ever dated," she said. "I guess I'm still trying to figure you out."

"Oh, don't be fooled," Shenin said, "if anyone actually lays a hand on you in my presence they're going to be really sorry," this was said with the sweetest smile, and Tyler realized that maybe she didn't quite know Shenin as well as she thought. In some strange way it kind of excited her.

CHAPTER 10

Tyler got to see Shenin's possessive streak a few days later. Tyler had been working out at the Base gym. She was just coming out of the locker room, her hair in wet curls from her shower. She was dressed in her jeans, boots and a black button up shirt, she was buttoning one of the sleeves as she walked out and she literally ran into someone she'd dated years before at Nellis.

"Tyler?" The girl said, as they both stepped back.

Tyler recognized the girl, she'd been a handful. "Hi, Jo."

"Wow, weird running into you here." Jo enthused. "You look great!"

"Thanks," Tyler said, nodding.

"Are you stationed here now?" Jo asked hopefully.

"Aw, no," Tyler said, glancing around, Shenin was supposed to be picking her up; she was hoping she was already there so she could escape this conversation. No such luck. "I'm still at Nellis."

"So, what are you doing here?" Jo asked.

"I'm, uh, visiting," Tyler said, not really wanting to get into a discussion with the girl. She remembered that the girl had been really clingy, and had been really unhappy when Tyler had broken it off. Like break all the windows in your car, unhappy.

"Oh, well," Jo said, shifting mental gears, "do you think we could get together?"

Tyler couldn't help herself. "Why?" she asked.

Jo looked sheepish for a moment, almost pulling it off. "I just wanted to maybe talk, we kind of parted ways badly."

"You trashed all the windows in my car," Tyler said, matter-of-factly, her look circumspect.

"I know," Jo said, reaching out to touch Tyler's arm, not seeming to notice when Tyler tensed, so Tyler gently pulled away. "I'm really sorry," she said, "I was a lot younger then, and I really didn't know how to handle a break up."

Tyler looked back at the girl for a long moment, then nodded. "Okay, well, it was a long time ago, so I think we can forget about it."

"That would be great!" Jo said, putting her hand on Tyler's arm again.

"Okay," Tyler said, stepping back, Jo followed, putting her other hand on Tyler's arm now too.

"Hi," Shenin said, walking up. She was in uniform, her lieutenant's bar shining in the lights of the gym. Jo, who was in uniform and only an airman, immediately let go of Tyler's arm and snapped to attention, saluting.

Shenin turned her head to look at the blond who'd been clutching Tyler's arm a moment before, and Tyler could literally see the heat coming out of her eyes. She waited to see how long Shenin would make Jo sweat before she returned her salute. Shenin's eyes skipped from the blond over to Tyler, who was grinning and shaking her head, then her eyes settled back on Jo. Slowly she reached up and returned the girl's salute. Jo dropped her hand, but remained at attention because Shenin hadn't given her an "at ease" yet.

"Who's your friend, Ty?" Shenin asked, her tone falsely light.

Tyler actually felt sorry for Jo at that point. "Joanne Keely, Lieutenant Shenin Devereaux, Shen, this is Joanne."

Shenin nodded, slowly, her look measuring at Jo. "And she was grabbing at you, why?" she asked, her tone conversational, but her gold eyes were shooting sparks.

"She was asking for forgiveness for a past transgression," Tyler said, "no big deal."

"I see," Shenin said, her look considering, her eyes skimmed back to Jo then. "At ease, airman," she said.

Tyler thought Jo was actually going to pass out, it was endlessly amusing.

"You ready?" Shenin asked Tyler brightly, ignoring the girl altogether.

"Yeah," Tyler said, nodding.

"Shall we?" Shenin said, gesturing for Tyler to lead the way, glancing at Jo as Tyler walked by her. Shenin pointedly reached out to take Tyler's hand firmly in hers. "Dismissed, airman," she said to Jo, as she turned and walked away.

Joanne stared after them in complete shock.

"Wow…" Tyler said when they reached the car.

"What?" Shenin asked, looking completely innocent.

"Is that what you're like when you get all possessive?" Tyler asked.

"She's lucky I walked up when I did," Shenin said mildly. "I'm sure she needs her hands for something."

Tyler looked back at this woman she'd known for almost two years, and wondered if she'd ever totally known her. Getting to know this side of Shenin was an exciting prospect.

Later that night, they were having dinner out for a change, and they talked more about Jo, and other things.

"So, she actually smashed all the windows in your car?" Shenin asked, stunned.

"Yep," Tyler said, "cost me a damned fortune to replace them all."

Shenin shook her head. "I let the bitch off too easy."

"Oh, I think you scared the crap out of her," Tyler said. "She's terrified of officers."

Shenin chuckled. "That's good to know," her eyes sparkling maliciously.

"You can be downright evil, I see that now." Tyler said, grinning.

“I told you, if people put their hands on something or someone that belongs to me, I’m not exactly a nice person about it.”

“So I belong to you now?” Tyler asked, raising an eyebrow.

“Oh, I’m sorry, was that somehow unclear?” Shenin replied, raising an eyebrow in response.

“It might have been,” Tyler replied, grinning.

“Well, let’s make this crystal clear then,” Shenin said. “You are mine, and I’ll take on anyone that tries to say different, including you.”

Tyler nodded slowly. “Got it.”

“Good,” Shenin replied. “So, exactly how many women have you dated, Tyler?” She asked then, her voice emphasizing the words ‘how many’.

Tyler grinned rakishly at that point. “I guess, a lot more than I thought,” she answered, looking somewhat aghast.

“I mean, how many more are we going to run into here in the wastelands of Alaska?”

Tyler laughed. “Hopefully not too many more,” she replied. “You gottta understand that the lesbian community in the military isn’t really that big. And when you’ve been around as long as I have, and out for as long as I have, you tend to rack up some frequent flyer miles.”

Shenin burst out laughing. “Frequent flyer miles?” she repeated.

“Yeah.” Tyler grinned, her blue eyes twinkling. “Not liking that whole other women after your woman thing so much now, are ya?”

"Ya know..." Shenin said, her voice trailing off ominously.

"Yes?" Tyler challenged with a grin.

"Oh shut up," Shenin said, giving her a dirty look. Tyler only laughed.

Later they were back at Shenin's house. Shenin went into the bathroom to change and take off her make-up. Tyler found that she was a little bit sore from her work out, and far too lazy to change clothes completely. So she took her boots and jeans off and lay down on the bed.

When Shenin came out of the bathroom she saw Tyler lying on the bed, her lanky frame looking highly attractive in her black shirt and not much else. She was lying with arm up over her head, her head resting on it.

Tyler looked up as Shenin walked into the room, her breath caught; Shenin was wearing nothing at all.

Blowing her breath out in a low whistle, Tyler grinned. "Now that's... wow," she said, shaking her head.

Shenin smiled, biting her lip, she hadn't been sure it was a good idea, but now seeing Tyler's response, she knew it had been a very good idea.

"C'mere," Tyler said, moving to sit up.

Shenin walked over to her, not sure what she was supposed to do at this point. Tyler reached up her hand, taking Shenin's hand and pulling her down on the bed and onto her lap. Reaching up to touch Shenin's face, Tyler stared up at her, then pulled her head down to kiss her deeply. Within minutes, they were both breathless. Shenin was grasping at Tyler's shoulders when their lips parted, she couldn't believe the sensations rushing through her.

"Wait, Ty," Shenin said, feeling Tyler's arms around her waist, her hands stroking her back. "Is this okay? Are you okay?"

Tyler grinned. "Well, I don't think I'd say okay, but yes, this is fine."

With that they kissed again, and within minutes they were making love, and there was no more talking until they both lay intertwined and breathless.

"Well," Shenin said, still trying to catch her breath and calm her pulse, "I think that the question of whether or not I'm sexually attracted to women has now been answered."

Tyler grinned. "And then some," she agreed.

Shenin's hand stroked Tyler's stomach, she'd unbuttoned Tyler's shirt during their frantic love making, but she hadn't taken it off. Shenin's eyes trailed down to the still healing scars on Tyler's chest. She touched them gently, looking up to see Tyler watching her. Without a word Shenin leaned in and kissed each mark on Tyler's skin that had been made by the IED. She felt Tyler's hand on her head as she did, when she glanced up, Tyler was smiling softly. Their eyes met, and Tyler was once again astounded by this woman.

Moving to sit up Tyler pulled off the shirt and lay back down, pulling Shenin into her arms.

“This feels so nice,” Shenin said, snuggling against Tyler’s side.

“Yeah, it does,” Tyler agreed.

Shenin let her eyes trail down Tyler’s body, the woman was definitely fit. When she got to Tyler’s hips she noticed something surprising. Tyler had a tattoo.

Leveraging herself up, Shenin examined the tattoo more closely: it was a dragon with green wings and a green and purple body. As she moved back to look at Tyler, she spotted a second tattoo on her upper left thigh. This tattoo was an Indian tomahawk with a braided handle.

“Why didn’t I know you had tattoos?” Shenin asked, her tone almost accusing.

Tyler grinned. “Uh, the subject never really came up.”

Shenin stared back at her for a long moment still shocked.

“What’s the big deal?” Tyler asked, looking amused.

“It’s not a big deal,” Shenin said, “I guess I’m just surprised.”

“Why surprised?” Tyler asked.

Shenin shrugged. “I don’t know, I guess I thought I knew a lot about you, and now I’m seeing that maybe I’m going to be getting to know you all over again.”

Tyler gave her a searching look. “You knew me on a friendship level, Shen,” she said. “An intimate level is a whole other thing.”

Shenin nodded, looking a little dismayed.

Tyler watched her for a long moment, then reached down tipping her face up to her again and kissing her lips. "If it helps," she said, "I've been a lot closer to the real me with you than I ever have with anyone else, friend or girlfriend."

"Really?" Shenin asked, hoping Tyler wasn't just saying that to make her feel better.

"Really, babe," Tyler said nodding, her look direct.

"So what have I missed?" Shenin asked, grinning.

"Well, there's the fun, possessive, jealous me," Tyler said.

"I've seen that," Shenin said.

Tyler laughed out loud at that. "Oh, no," she said, "you've only seen the tip of the iceberg on that one, babe."

"No way..." Shenin said, thinking that her calm, passive Tyler couldn't be a crazy jealous person.

Tyler looked back at her, seeing the look of disbelief on Shenin's face. "Okay, I'm not boil your bunny kind of crazy, no," she said, grinning again. "But I've been pretty low key up until this point."

"Hmmm," Shenin murmured, "really now?"

Tyler nodded.

"Well, we'll just see about that..." Shenin said, chuckling.

The next day, Tyler finally got to see Shenin doing her "cardio dance thing," as Tyler had started calling it. They went to a dance studio in the neighboring town. It was small, but there were a lot of women there. Shenin greeted a few of them. When she went up to sign in, Tyler was standing with her. There was a petite Latina sitting behind the table.

"Morning, Vanessa," Shenin said, smiling as she signed the book in front of her.

Vanessa smiled brightly at Shenin and then her eyes went to Tyler. "Who is your friend?" she asked, her accent prevalent and quite sassy as well. "And why isn't she dressed to dance with us?"

Shenin laughed. "Easy now," she said to Vanessa. "She's just gotten back from Iraq, where the Iraqis tried to blow her up. Give her a little bit of a break."

"Oh my God!" Vanessa said, looking back at Tyler again. "This is your friend? The one that was hurt?"

"This is my girlfriend," Shenin said, emphasizing the word "girlfriend." "Tyler Hancock, this is Vanessa. Vanessa this is Ty."

Vanessa extended her hand to Tyler, "It is really nice to meet you. I'm glad you're okay," she said, smiling, then her look turned mischievous. "I won't give you a hard time today, but next time you come, you come to dance." She said, her tone bossy.

"Yes, ma'am," Tyler responded with a grin.

Shenin went to find her place on the floor, glancing at Tyler standing behind the half wall separating the dance floor from the front of the Studio. She winked at Tyler, just as the music started and Vanessa called, "This is warm up!"

Tyler found herself fascinated by the class; it definitely looked like a good way to work out, as long as you had actual rhythm. Vanessa was a tiny little dynamo that Tyler found impossibly energetic. It was exhausting just watching the class. She also found that watching Shenin dance the way some of the routines called for was kind of hot and not in the sweaty way, although there seemed to be a lot of sweating going on too.

At the end of the class, Shenin came over, toweling off her face.

"What'd you think?" she asked, having seen Tyler watching the class the whole time.

"I think I know why you're in such good shape," Tyler said, grinning. "And I think that Vanessa is part rabbit as high as she jumps."

Shenin laughed. "I agree with that," she said, smiling, "I've called her the Energizer Bunny from Hell on several occasions."

Tyler laughed at that. "Sounds about right," she said, especially considering Vanessa didn't even look winded. It wasn't fair.

They left the studio, waving to Vanessa on their way out. She waved and gave them a big smile. "Remember!" she called to Tyler, "next time you don't get to be lazy!"

Tyler laughed, nodding her head.

Shenin finally got the opportunity to see Tyler's possessive streak two days later when they went out to the club. They went with Anne and her group of friends. Everything started off fine. Tyler held tightly to Shenin's hand when they walked into the club and found a table that would fit the group they made. As the club got busier, and drinks started to be consumed, things got a little crazier.

Tyler could see exactly what Anne meant about the women in the club zeroing in on Shenin. At one point Shenin went off to the bathroom, and when she was headed back, Tyler saw some woman step into her path. Tyler stood up, but saw that Shenin was shaking her head and getting around the woman with no problem. No point in getting into a fight she didn't need to get into. Tyler did note that the woman went back over to her friends and the group watched where she went. Tyler remained standing when Shenin got back to their table, her eyes on the group of women, Tyler pulled Shenin into her arms, kissing her deeply. Shenin seemed surprised, but responded by wrapping her arms around Tyler's neck and kissing her back just as deeply.

When their lips parted Shenin was grinning. "I assume we were just sending a message."

"You assume right," Tyler said, grinning right back at her.

"So hot!" said one of Anne's friends, a big butch girl named Tammy. She'd had plenty to drink so she was being a bit loud.

Tyler and Shenin just grinned and moved to sit back down. A little while later, Tyler headed to the bar to grab some more drinks, leaning in to kiss Shenin before she did.

"We'll keep an eye on her," Tammy slurred, reaching out to slide her hand down Shenin's arm.

Tyler raised an eyebrow, and glanced over at Anne. Anne made a gesture like she was drinking from a bottle to indicate that Tammy had drunk too much. Tyler nodded, and rolling her eyes at Shenin she left the group.

"How does somebody so hot like you get stuck in the Air Force," Tammy said, sliding over to sit way too close to Shenin. Shenin shifted imperceptibly to at least back away from the alcohol fumes Tammy was emitting.

"Joined up, just like everyone else," Shenin joked, trying to diffuse the whole thing.

"Nah." Tammy shook her head. "That's just wrong," she said, leaning really close again, "you should be like a model or something not some fuckin' first lewy."

Shenin glanced at Anne, who was looking decidedly nervous suddenly.

"Thanks," Shenin said, getting up to get away from Tammy before Tyler got back. Tammy, however, didn't like that and made the mistake of grabbing Shenin's wrist.

Tyler was there instantly, and to Shenin she was suddenly much bigger than she normally was. "Get your hand off her, now," Tyler said, her tone no nonsense.

"S'okay man," Tammy slurred, "the lewy and I were talkin'. Just chill."

Tyler's eyes took on a more dangerous look at that point. "I'm telling you again, and you better be listening this time, get your hand off of her."

"Jesus!" Tammy exploded, standing up suddenly and getting in Tyler's face, letting go of Shenin in the process. "What is your fuckin' problem!"

Tammy was as tall as Tyler, and about a foot wider, she worked in the mechanical crew, so she was pretty solid in the muscle department.

Tyler looked back at the other woman, not the least bit intimidated, even though Tammy was literally an inch from her face.

"My problem is your putting your hands on my girl," Tyler explained simply, her blue eyes staring back into Tammy's.

"Your girl," Tammy said, her tone mocking. "Ain't we all fighting for this free country? What makes you think she didn't like it?" she said then, grinning.

Tammy looked around her, expecting back up from her friends, not realizing that they were all sitting tensely waiting to see what was going to happen. Tammy didn't see it, what she did next was nearly fatal, she reached out to grab at Shenin again.

Tyler reacted instantly, reaching out, she grabbed the wrist attached to the hand that was moving toward Shenin. Yanking Tammy's hand toward her and twisting in the same motion, Tyler pulled Tammy's arm up behind her back, and with that momentum, slammed her face down on the table. She then leaned down over the struggling woman and said, "I warned you."

"Get the fuck off me!" Tammy screamed, struggling against Tyler's hold.

Tammy was stronger than Tyler gave her credit for, and managed to kick out trying to kick her in the knee. Tyler had to let her go to jump back out of the way. Tammy, surprising agile for her size turned around and grabbed at Tyler, punching her in the face and shoving her to the ground.

"Tyler!" Shenin yelled, moving toward the two women, but Tammy was already tackling Tyler to the floor.

Tyler knew better than to end up under the heavier woman, so she shifted as they were falling using a booted foot to shove against Tammy to give herself some room to maneuver. She quickly rolled to her feet, taking on a fighter's stance. Tammy was shocked to end up on the floor without Tyler under her, scrambling up off the ground; she turned to face Tyler again. Tyler's blue eyes were blazing, now she wasn't just protecting Shenin, now she was mad. Foolishly, Tammy gave some kind of insane banshee cry as she launched herself at Tyler, it was the warning Tyler needed to step out of the way of Tammy's advancing bulk. Tammy's momentum carried her past Tyler who put out a booted foot to catch her in the stomach, and followed through with a punch to the other woman's jaw. Tammy collapsed on the ground, coughing.

Shenin was next to Tyler immediately, Tyler put her arm out to bar Shenin from getting too close. She stood panting, and watching to make sure Tammy didn't get back up, the last thing she wanted was for Shenin to get caught in the middle if Tammy tried anything else. She tasted blood, and reaching up she touched her lip, pulling back her hand she saw that she was indeed bleeding. When she was sure

Tammy was done, Tyler relaxed and Shenin was there immediately her arm around her supporting her weight.

“I’m okay,” Tyler said, her voice ragged from the gasping breaths she was taking.

Shenin sat her down and looked at her face, her eyes worried. “Oh God, Ty…” she said, touching the bruise that was already starting on her jaw.

Tyler flinched when Shenin touched the cut, pulling her head back, “I’m okay,” she repeated.

Anne was there then. “I’m so sorry, Tyler, I don’t know what she thought she was doing.”

Tyler eyed Tammy as Anne’s other friends helped her get up. “You mean besides being a drunken dumb ass?”

“Yeah,” Anne said, nodding, looking really embarrassed.

Security walked up then, and Shenin took charge. She explained to the guards what happened, and that Tammy had attacked Tyler and she’d only been defending herself. Anne’s friends backed up Shenin’s statements, even as two of them supported a very groggy Tammy.

“Get her out of here,” the security guard told the women hold Tammy up. They nodded and walked away with Tammy in tow. “You okay?” one of the guards asked Tyler.

Tyler nodded. The guards walked away then. Everyone was left to what was left of their night. Shenin had no idea what to think about what had happened. She’d never had anyone defend her like Tyler just had. She felt horrible that Tyler had been hurt in the process.

"Let's get you home," Shenin said to Tyler, her eyes worried.

Tyler glanced at her, seeing the look of worry, she immediately reached up touching Shenin's cheek, "I'm okay, babe," she told her, "I've come out worse in a wrestling match with Sheila."

Shenin laughed softly, nodding.

"I'm just going to go clean up," she said, standing.

Shenin stood at the same time, and in answer to Tyler's quizzical look said, "You don't think I'm letting you out of my sight after that, do you?"

Tyler grinned, then winced when it hurt her mouth.

As they were walking to the bathroom, Shenin noticed that Tyler was getting not only a lot of nods of respect, but also a lot of more amorous looks. By the time they got to the bathroom Shenin was shaking her head.

"Jesus!" she said, rolling her eyes. "Now I'm going to have to fight my way out of here!"

"Oh stop," Tyler said, laughing.

Walking over to the sink Shenin grabbed some paper towels and wet them. "Come here," she said, putting her back to the sink, leaning against it.

Tyler walked over to her, standing in front of her, putting her hands on Shenin's hips. As Shenin dabbed gently a Tyler's lip, two women walked into the bathroom.

“Bad ass fight,” one said, to Tyler, looking at her reflection in the mirror.

“You were awesome,” said the other girl.

“Thanks,” Tyler said, garnering a dirty look from Shenin who was still trying to get the blood off her lips. “Sorry,” she murmured, repressing a grin.

“You two a thing?” the second girl asked.

Shenin gave the girl a look that said, *Really?* “Yes, we are,” she said.

“That’s cool,” the girl replied. “So your woman stuck up for, that’s pretty awesome, right?”

Shenin’s eyes flicked to connect with Tyler’s and then back at the girl. “Yeah, it’s pretty awesome,” she said, repeating the girl’s words, looking back at Tyler she grinned.

“Pretty little thing like you probably needs protection,” the girl continued, her tone condescending.

Tyler closed her eyes, thinking, *son of a bitch…*

Shenin clicked her tongue as she did her best to remember she was an officer in the US Air Force and it wouldn’t do well to get into trouble beating the shit out of some snide little bitch in a night club.

When Tyler opened her eyes, she saw the look in Shenin’s eyes.

Turning, she put her back to Shenin, leaning back against her and looking at the girl.

"You might want to be careful," Tyler told the girl, "she may seem beautiful and helpless, but she's far from it. So could you please just give us a break tonight?"

The girl considered this. Shenin, who was the same height as Tyler that evening due to the heels she was wearing, put her arms on Tyler's shoulders, gold eyes issuing a warning to the girl from behind Tyler.

Fortunately, for everyone involved the first girl decided that both women were probably not to be tangled with so she pulled her friend out of the bathroom. Tyler and Shenin laughed, after the door closed.

"It's really dangerous going out with you," Tyler observed later that night on the way home. She was driving Shenin's car.

"Me?" Shenin said, "look who's talking! Those girls weren't in that bathroom because you're some slouch in the looks department, babe."

"Uh-huh," Tyler said, grinning, "you did really well at controlling yourself in there. I'm proud of you."

"Bite me," Shenin said, giving her a vile look. "If I wasn't an officer I would have shown that little bitch a thing or two about being 'beautiful and helpless'."

"She wasn't worth your commission, babe," Tyler said.

"Uh-huh, I know that, that's why she's still breathing."

Tyler looked over at Shenin, grinning. "So tough," she said.

"I'll show you tough," Shenin said, narrowing her eyes at Tyler.

Later back at the house, Shenin did something that shocked Tyler to her very core. While they were making love, Shenin moved over her, pressing her body against Tyler's and moving suggestively. Tyler was completely stunned by her reaction to this, her body lit up, when Shenin went to move, Tyler held her fast, "Don't move," she said, her voice ragged. She then proceeded to coax Shenin to move with her, within minutes they were both crying out. They lay breathing heavily with Shenin still over Tyler, Tyler's hands caressing her back.

"Well, that's a first," Tyler said, grinning in the semi-darkness of the room.

"What?" Shenin asked, her voice breathless.

"No one's ever topped me before," Tyler said simply.

Shenin looked perplexed. "What?" she asked.

Tyler grinned. "Uh, it's a lesbian term, it basically means the one who took control here," she said, gesturing between them.

"Oh," Shenin said, "and no one else has ever done that to you before?"

"One girl tried, once, didn't work," Tyler said.

"But, this did?" Shenin asked, trying to ask without sounding dumb.

"Oh yes, this did," Tyler said, smiling.

Shenin smiled. "Well then," she said, widening her eyes.

Tyler shook her head. "I'm not sure if you'll ever stop shocking the shit out of me," she told her honestly.

"I'll keep you on your toes," Shenin said.

"You always have," Tyler agreed.

"Mmmm," Shenin said, leaning in to kiss her again. They made love a few more times that night.

CHAPTER 11

All too quickly, the month was up and Tyler was preparing to leave for Nellis to finish up a few things before she went on to OTS in Alabama. Tyler and Shenin spent their last night at home, spending as much time together as they could. Shenin had told Tyler everything she could think of about Officer Training School. Tyler was finally feeling normal and felt like she could actually handle the rigors of the program.

The morning Tyler took off, Shenin walked her to the flight line. The transport Tyler was taking was sitting on the tarmac and other soldiers were boarding.

"I better go," Tyler said, turning to Shenin and setting her duffel down on the ground, taking Shenin's face in her hands, knowing she was taking a risk. "I will call you as often as I can," she told Shenin.

Shenin nodded, feeling really emotional at that point, she knew that it may be months and months before she saw Tyler again, especially if she received a post that was really far away.

Tyler's eyes searched Shenin's. "You still with me?" she asked.

Shenin nodded again. "Yes," she said softly, tears in her eyes.

"Oh babe," Tyler said, pulling her into her arms and hugging her close. "I love you." she whispered, "I'll do everything I can to get some leave after OTS and we can do something, okay?"

Shenin once again nodded, against Tyler's chest. "Okay," she said, her voice muffled by Tyler's jacket. She lifted her head looking up into Tyler's eyes, "I love you, be safe."

Tyler smiled down at her, leaning down and kissing her softly on the lips. Letting her go, she stepped back and picked up her duffle, slinging it over her shoulder. She began walking toward the plane, turning around and waving to Shenin one last time. Shenin waved back, wanting desperately to run after her and keep her from leaving.

Twenty minutes later, Shenin watched as the transport taxied and took off. She watched until the plane was completely out of sight and then she turned and went to the squad room. Locking herself in her office she cried for twenty minutes; it was all the time she'd allow herself.

After that she went back to work, bound and determined that she was going to handle this separation right, not go all to pieces. She found over the next couple of weeks that she needed to fill her evenings, lest she lay in bed and think of when she was spending time with Tyler there. Tyler called her the first night of OTS.

"How's it going over there?" Shenin asked, making herself sound cheerful.

"It's alright," Tyler said, lying back in her bunk, she was looking up at the picture she had of Shenin taped to the underside of the bunk above her. "I miss you," she said simply.

Shenin sighed. "I miss you too, babe," she said.

"Nine weeks," Tyler said, "we survived a lot longer than that before."

"Yes, I know," Shenin said, but wanted to say, *but that was before I got so completely used to your body next to me at night!* But she didn't say that, it wouldn't do either of them any good. Shenin knew that Tyler needed to be able to focus on her courses and her studies, the last thing she needed was a whiney girlfriend, so she wasn't going to be one.

The next morning there was a knock on her office door. "Come!" Shenin called, Anne opened the door, and came to attention saluting.

Shenin returned the salute. "Come on in," she said, nodding.

"How're you doing?" Anne asked, seeing that Shenin seemed very subdued.

"I miss her like crazy," Shenin said, honestly, "but it is what it is, right? I may as well get used to this."

Anne frowned. "I'm sorry."

Shenin nodded.

A week into OTS Tyler finally felt like she was getting the hang of everything. She was getting into the rhythm of the place. She had a roommate in the barracks: her name was Crystal Limon. Crystal was from Texas, and had the personality to match. She and Tyler got along pretty well. Crystal was missing her boyfriend in Texas, and Tyler was missing Shenin.

"So, she's your girlfriend?" Crystal asked one night early on.

Tyler nodded, her grin in place, Crystal didn't seem to understand the concept of gay, Tyler wasn't sure why.

"So, like, y'all are dating?" Crystal clarified.

"Right," Tyler said, nodding.

"Is she enlisted personnel?"

"No, she's a lieutenant," Tyler said.

"Then how are y'all dating, you aren't an officer yet," Crystal asked as if it was impossible to break regulations.

Tyler just looked back at her for a moment. "Trust me, it's possible," she said, thinking that it was going to be fun dealing with her for nine full weeks.

"Well, how does that work, you know, sexually," Crystal asked then, waving her hand in Tyler's direction.

Tyler chuckled. "It works just fine, thanks."

"But ya can't have a wienie roast without no dogs," Crystal said, looking completely oblivious.

Tyler laughed out loud at that one. "We prefer tacos," she said, which completely mystified Crystal.

"But what's your goal there?" Crystal asked.

"Goal?" Tyler asked, quite amused by this line of questioning.

"You know," Crystal said, "like the point?"

Tyler rubbed the bridge of her nose with her forefinger. "You mean, the main goal of sex?"

"Well, like gay sex, yeah."

"Technically it's just called sex, but it's pretty much the same goal everyone else has when they have sex."

"But y'all can't make kids, two cows with no bull, ya know?" Crystal said, sounding very Texan.

"Well, yes, I know," Tyler said, blinking and trying to suppress her grin. "But do you only have sex with Wyatt to have kids?"

"Well, no," Crystal said, looking at her as if she was crazy, "we have sex 'cause it's fun!"

Again Tyler looked at her for a long minute unable to figure out how this person actually got into Officer Training School, but it seemed that her ignorance only seemed to be for this subject at this point.

"Sex is fun for us too," Tyler told her simply.

"How 'bout that," Crystal said, smiling her big toothy smile.

Tyler shook her head, and said, "I'm going to make a call," and she walked out of the room and out the door of the barracks.

Shenin answered on the second ring, Tyler regaled her with Crystal's questions, which had them both laughing for a good fifteen minutes.

Tyler and Crystal were the only two women in their particular group, and Tyler found out quickly that the men in their unit did not like the idea of any woman doing better than them. When it came to hand-to-hand combat, Tyler noted that the men pulled no punches, which for her was just fine, but it did mean she got back to the barracks bruised and battered on a few occasions.

One such occasion was a night when she talked to Shenin. For once Crystal wasn't in the room so she had the option of talking to Shenin while lying in her bunk. Since she really didn't feel like moving, it was a time she was grateful for.

While they talked, Tyler shifted, groaning as her body protested the shift.

"Ty?" Shenin queried immediately. "What's wrong?"

"Oh, I'm sporting a couple of fairly nasty bruises from today," she replied, knowing that it had been a mistake to make the noise in the first place.

"Why? What happened?" Shenin asked, sounding worried.

"Nothing, babe, I'm fine, just a couple of my teammates getting a little over zealous during hand-to-hand."

"You're supposed to be learning techniques, not beating the hell out of each other." Shenin said, sounding frustrated.

"Yeah, well," Tyler said, making the mistake of shrugging. "Take red-blooded, beef-fed, American farm boys with machismo coming out their ears, add a lesbian who's obviously better at hand-to-hand than they are, and the double teaming seems to become the order of the day."

"That's ridiculous!" Shenin snapped, "they can't get away with that Tyler," she said, really upset now.

"Shen," Tyler said, trying to break through her rant, "it's okay, they're just bruises, I'm fine."

"Sons a bitches," Shenin sputtered angrily.

"Yes, yes they are," Tyler agreed, grinning that her girl was so very protective, even from forty-two hundred miles away.

"Is nine weeks over yet?" Shenin asked petulantly.

"Not, quite, babe," Tyler said, "but we've only got five weeks to go."

"Okay," Shenin said, sighing. "At least I know I can be at your graduation," she said, smiling.

"Speaking of which," Tyler said. "Have you thought about doing something on the week between my leave and my report date?"

"I'll go anywhere you want me to go, Ty," Shenin said.

"I was thinking about Sacramento," Tyler said.

"You want me to take you home for your celebration for graduating?" Shenin said, sounding like that was a terrible idea.

"I haven't met anyone in your family," Tyler said.

"That'll take a minute," Shenin said. "I'm not quite the family person that you are, babe."

"I want to meet them, I want to see where you grew up," Tyler said.

"Okay," Shenin said, sounding resigned. "But Sacramento is boring as Hell, why do you think I joined the Force?"

"To meet me," Tyler said, sounding sure.

Shenin smiled on her end. "Okay, maybe for that too."

"Oh, speaking of family, I talked to mine," Tyler said.

"Okay," Shenin said, not sure where Tyler was headed with that conversation. "You talk to them all the time."

"I told them about you and me," Tyler said.

"Oh," Shenin said, grimacing, "how did that go?"

"Shen," Tyler said, her tone indicating that Shenin was worried unnecessarily. "They loved you, and they're really happy to hear we're together."

"They are?" Shenin asked, surprised.

"My dad's so excited that I'm in Officer Training School, and that was all you, babe."

"It was not," Shenin said. "You applied, you qualified, you're there doing the work."

"Yeah, but I never would have done it if I hadn't been wanting to avoid the fraternizing rule. I did this for you, babe, all for you."

Tyler glanced up, noticing that Crystal had come into the room.

Tyler sighed. "I gotta get goin' babe," she said. "I have some homework to do before I go to bed."

"Okay, try to put some ice on those bruises, and be careful!"

"I will," Tyler said, smiling. "I love you," she said then, her voice as soft as ever when she did.

"I love you," Shenin replied.

When Tyler hung up, she noticed that Crystal was staring at her with a canted head. Tyler had learned that when Crystal did that, it was because she had something to say. Tyler prepared herself for another round of "why do you wanna be gay?"

"That's nice," Crystal said, surprising Tyler.

"What is?" Tyler asked, rubbing at her arm.

"That you tell your gal you love her," Crystal said, her tone somewhat wistful. "Do you do that a lot?"

"Every chance I get," Tyler said, trying to figure out where Crystal was coming from this time.

Crystal looked considering, then sighed. "I wish Wyatt would tell me he loves me all the time."

Tyler nodded, maybe being straight wasn't so easy either.

Before they knew it, Tyler was graduating from Officer Training School. Shenin, Sheila, Jean and Tyler's parents flew in for the ceremony. Because she wanted to make sure she got to the graduation in plenty of time, Shenin opted for flying commercially from Fairbanks, Alaska to Montgomery, Alabama. Tyler and her parents picked her up at the airport.

Carl and Becky noticed that their daughter paced more than she ever had before. Wearing her dress uniform, Tyler looked every bit the Air Force officer, her parents were extremely proud of her. And from what Tyler had told them, it was the prospect of being able to date Shenin without fear of fraternization issues, which had prompted her to apply to Officer Training School. If that was the case, they liked the petite redhead all the more.

As Shenin's plane arrived, they could see Tyler's impatience at seeing her girlfriend. When Shenin got off the plane she wasn't wearing her uniform. When she saw Tyler, she smiled so brightly and ran up to her. Tyler grabbed Shenin up in her arms, holding her close and hugging her. Setting her back on her feet, Tyler looked down at Shenin and leaned down to kiss her tenderly on the lips.

Moving her lips to Shenin's ear, she whispered, "I missed you."

Shenin pulled back to look at her, taking Tyler's face in her hands. "I missed you," she said, kissing her again, careful to make sure they didn't overdo it, since Tyler was in uniform.

Neither of them noticed people all around them watching and smiling. It was so obvious to anyone watching that these two were in love, and now that Don't Ask, Don't Tell had been abolished, love like this could be displayed. Just like any other soldier welcoming a loved one, or the other way around. Carl and Becky watched as well, impressed with the amount of tenderness between their daughter and Shenin. Maybe Tyler being gay wasn't something they completely understood, but they knew when their daughter was in love, and there was no way they could not appreciate that.

Tyler turned, taking Shenin's hand and leading her over to her parents.

"Hi!" Shenin said, smiling from ear to ear. "You made it, I'm so happy!" she said, knowing that it had been really important to Tyler that her parents make it. She wanted so much for them to be proud of her, and because Tyler wanted that more than anything, Shenin wanted it for her.

Carl opened his arms to Shenin, and she happily moved into them to hug him. Becky hugged her next, giving her an extra squeeze.

"Good flight?" Becky asked Shenin, as they headed to baggage claim.

"Long," Shenin said. "but still way better than a transport," she said, winking at Tyler.

"Yeah," Tyler said, "and way more expensive."

"It's worth it, I wanted to make sure I made it in plenty of time, you know how the transports get," Shenin said, smiling.

"Okay, so let me pay for it," Tyler said.

"Not gonna happen," Shenin replied with an amused light in her eyes that told Carl and Becky this was an ongoing discussion.

Tyler narrowed her eyes at Shenin. "You wouldn't have had to come all the way here, if I wasn't graduating," she reasoned.

Shenin narrowed her eyes right back. “Tell you what,” she said, smiling sweetly. “You give me, oh, three or four months’ of those cell phone bills you made calling me from Iraq, and we can discuss my plane fare.”

“Not gonna happen,” Tyler replied, repeating Shenin’s words.

“Then shut up,” Shenin replied, just as sweetly, batting her eyelashes.

Tyler made a face at her, and Shenin stuck her tongue out at her. Tyler’s parents had to admit, that Shenin certainly knew how to handle Tyler. Even before she’d discovered she was gay, Tyler had always dominated her relationships. It didn’t seem to be the case here, they actually seemed to be equals.

Everyone was staying at a hotel in Montgomery, not too far from the base. Tyler drove them all back to the hotel and carried Shenin’s bags to her room. They arranged to meet Tyler’s parents later that evening for dinner.

Once in the room, Tyler pulled Shenin to her, kissing her with what she considered a more proper “hello”. They kissed until they were breathless, and then Tyler was carrying her into the bedroom portion of the room. Before long, clothes were on the floor, or carefully laid over a chair in Tyler’s uniform’s case, and they were making love.

Lying together afterward, Shenin lay curled in Tyler’s arms, feeling absolutely wonderful. It was amazing to her how good it felt to be with Tyler, how natural, like it had always meant to be that way.

"Does it always feel this way for you?" Shenin asked, glancing up at Tyler.

"What do you mean?" Tyler asked.

"I mean, well, for me, this feels like I've always been meant to be here with you. I'm just curious if this is what it felt like when you were with a woman for the first time."

Tyler looked back at her for a long moment, her eyes searching Shenin's. She was looking for a sign that Shenin was kidding, but it didn't look like she was.

"Shen, I've never felt this way with anyone else," she said, her tone serious. "No one has ever made me feel the way you do, no one."

Shenin stared up at Tyler, her look surprised.

"You need to know," Tyler said, reaching out to touch Shenin's face gently, "that this kind of thing doesn't happen all the time. This is what most lesbians would kill to find. They'll search their whole lives to find this, and never find it. "

"Wow," Shenin said, honestly surprised by what Tyler was saying. "So us finding each other the way we did, that's not common?"

"Well," Tyler said, grinning. "The way we found each other was crazy, since ya know, we're in the Air Force and all, and strictly forbidden from being gay up until about six months ago."

Shenin chuckled. "Yeah, I guess that would be true, huh?"

"Lil' bit," Tyler said, winking.

"Lil' bit," Shenin replied, grinning.

"I guess I never really told you how different this is for me, have I?" Tyler asked.

"Well, no," Shenin said, "but technically we've only really been together for three months, it might have taken that long for you to see it."

Tyler snorted sardonically. "Oh babe, I've felt like this about you since the day we met." She said, "I guess it didn't really occur to me that you wouldn't know that. I never get into fights over women, I never go out of my way to be with someone who is probably going to only cause me trouble. Like a straight woman, who's also military and an officer."

Shenin pressed her lips together, her eyes twinkling. "So, you kinda like me, huh?"

"Lil' bit," Tyler said again.

"Lil' bit," Shenin repeated, winking at her.

They spent the next couple of hours showing each other how much they loved each other. Sheila and Jean recognized that after sex glow at dinner, grinning about it. They were having dinner in the hotel restaurant. When Becky and Carl joined them, Jean found it necessary to tell them about how Tyler had saved her life.

"Your daughter is amazing," Jean told them. "She saved my life, and it almost cost her hers. You should be really proud of her."

"We are," Becky assured Jean. "I'm really glad that you're alright, and that Tyler healed well too," she said, reaching over to squeeze her daughter's hand.

"Shenin helped that," Sheila put in. "She got to Germany within a day of the incident. She gave Tyler an order that she wasn't allowed to die," Sheila said, grinning. "You listened to that order, didn't you, Ty?"

"Don't' make me kill you," Tyler said to Sheila, then to her parents she said, "Shenin's presence did make a big difference for me," she told them honestly. "And she did not order me not to die, she told me that she loved me and that she couldn't lose me." She said, taking Shenin's hand, "How could I ignore that?"

"I'm really glad you didn't," Shenin said, smiling.

"Me too," Tyler said, smiling back at her.

"Kinda like me huh?" Shenin said, repeating what they'd said earlier.

"Lil' bit," Tyler said, winking at her.

"Honestly, though," Sheila said. "Tyler is one of the best soldiers I've ever served with."

"Tyler always excels at whatever she does," Carl said, his tone proud. "Even in softball when she was a kid. If she missed a ball during a game, she'd practice for hours to try and ensure that it wouldn't happen again."

"Had nothing to do with the fact that my dad was the coach," Tyler said, grinning.

"Of course not," Carl said, winking at his daughter. The two shared a private smile. Shenin watched them, her smile warm. It made her so happy to see Tyler and her father getting along so well. She had no idea what it had been like prior to Tyler coming out, but she felt like they were talking much more comfortably even since the last time when they'd been in Maryland.

She mentioned it back in the room later that night. "Or am I crazy?" she asked, when she saw Tyler's smile, which only got wider when she asked that question. "What?" she asked then.

"You just surprise me sometimes," Tyler said, "with the way that you see things, and pay attention to things."

Shenin shrugged. "I just thought that your relationship with your father seemed good," she said.

"I know," Tyler said, "and you're right, it is, it's even better now than it was back when we were there. What surprises me is that you see that," she said.

"Anyone paying attention would see it, Ty." Shenin said.

"No," Tyler said, shaking her head, "not true. No one has ever been so interested in me that they care about my parents or my feelings, or what I want out of life. But you do, you care about all of it," she said, sounding awed.

Shenin furrowed her brow, trying to understand what Tyler was saying. "Tyler, I love you, and that means caring about everything about you, that's just part of that."

Tyler reached out, touching Shenin's face, "Well, it's amazing." She touched her thumb to Shenin's lips. "You are amazing."

"No," Shenin insisted, "I'm in love."

"Good thing," Tyler said, grinning. "'Cause I'm kinda in love with you too."

"Good thing," Shenin echoed.

Tyler's graduation day dawned a bright and beautiful day. The temperatures were in the low sixties, and the sky was as blue as it could be. Tyler left the hotel early to get back to her barracks and get ready for graduation. Shenin, Sheila, Jean, Carl, and Becky were heading to the graduation together after breakfast.

Shenin got to the restaurant first; Carl and Becky got there next. It was the chance they'd been waiting for.

"Before the other girls get here," Carl said to Shenin, "Becky and I wanted to talk to you."

Shenin looked at both of them, then nodded. "Okay," she said, her tone somewhat hesitant as she wasn't sure what they wanted to talk about.

Becky touched Shenin's arm, smiling. "Don't worry, we aren't going to bite."

Shenin smiled. "Good to know, I don't have my Kevlar on this morning."

Shenin was dressed in the blues of an officer, her First Lieutenant's silver bar shining.

Carl grinned. "Let's sit down," he said, gesturing to the table near them.

Sitting down, Carl took Shenin's hands in his. "We want you to know that we are so grateful to you for all that you've done for our daughter," he said sincerely.

"We've never seen her this happy," Becky said, "never. And when we heard what you went through to get to her in Germany," Becky said. "Sheila told us that you traveled for over a day and a half to get to Tyler," she said, then tears shining in her eyes as she did.

"Tyler never wanted to be an officer," Carl told Shenin. "She said that it was for others to lead, that she just wanted to be the best soldier she could." Carl said, looking a chagrinned, "I honestly think she didn't want to be an officer because she knew I never became one, I don't think she wanted to show up her old man."

"Tyler loves you two so much," Shenin told them, looking at each of them. "I can't begin to tell you what it must mean to her for you both to be here today. I know it's so important for her to make you both proud, but especially you," she said, looking at Carl.

"She's always been a daddy's girl," Becky said, smiling.

Shenin smiled nodding. "I know, I could see it when we were at the house that time."

"Was she telling us the truth then? Were you two just friends then?" Becky asked, then quickly followed up with, "Not that it matters, I'm just curious."

"Your daughter is very honest," Shenin said, "and yes, we were just friends then. In fact, I had just found out she was gay about an hour before we got to the house."

"Did she know you were gay?" Becky asked.

"I wasn't," Shenin said honestly.

"But…" Carl began, his voice trailing off as he couldn't think of a way to ask the question he wanted to without being disrespectful.

"And no, she didn't turn me gay," Shenin said. "Well, come to think of it, I guess she did."

"How?" Becky asked, looking like she thought that was impossible.

"By being herself," Shenin said, "by being kind and caring and sweet and gallant."

"Gallant?" Carl echoed.

Shenin smiled. "Tyler is very gallant, Mr. Hancock. She opens doors for me, she picks up my bags, she refuses to let me pay for anything, including her cell phone bill when she called me from Iraq, or offers to pay for my ticket to come here," she said. Her smile was even more fond as she said, "Or leaves a date to come sit with me during a thunderstorm because she knows they freak me out."

Becky was smiling, nodding her head. "She does sound like you Carl," she told him, "she grew up seeing you do those things, and now she does them too."

"Tyler is the most incredible person I've ever met," Shenin told them, "and I love her more than I ever thought I could love anyone."

"And we can see that," Becky said. "And we can see how she feels about you, and that is what we wanted to talk to you about."

"Okay," Shenin said, still not sure what to expect.

"We want to tell you that we'd be happy to consider you a daughter," Carl said, smiling warmly.

Shenin's eyes filled with tears. "Thank you," she said simply, nodding.

And just like his daughter would, Carl reached up and brushed away a tear with his thumb.

Shenin laughed then. "Tyler does that too."

Carl and Becky laughed too.

The graduation ceremony was a fairly formal affair. All of the officers were lined up in their "flights," the group they'd trained with during their time at OTS. They marched into view, their Parade Blue making them look very distinguished, especially with the white gloves they wore. Shenin saw Tyler, and felt her heart swell with pride. During the ceremony, there was the awarding of the Honor Flight Streamer, and it went to Tyler's flight for "excellence in academics, physical agility and overall performance."

Glancing at Tyler's parents, Shenin could see how impressed they were, and proud. She made a point of taking a picture of them beaming with pride for Tyler. When the flights were presented for review, Shenin, Sheila and Jean, all being in uniform, stood to watch Tyler's flight pass by. They all three saluted, and Shenin caught Tyler's quick grin. Later as the American flag passed, all military personnel in uniform stood at attention and saluted as was proper.

During the oath, Shenin remembered her oath taking and smiled fondly. At the end of the oath the new officers were told "Officers you are dismissed!" With that most of the officers cheered and tossed their caps in the air. Onlookers were then told they could join the graduates on the parade field. The group made its way to the field, looking for Tyler, having to stop and salute more than a few officers.

When they got to Tyler, she was talking to another girl that Shenin quickly identified as Crystal, from what Tyler had described. She walked up, giving Tyler and Crystal a salute, then leaning in to hug Tyler warmly.

"You did it!" she said, happily.

Sheila, Jean, Carl and Becky hugged her next.

"This must be Mrs. Tyler," Crystal said, looking at Shenin.

Tyler grinned inclining her head. "This is Shenin, Shen, this is Crystal."

Shenin extended her hand to the other woman. "It's nice to meet you, Tyler's told me a lot about you."

"Well, she hasn't told me a lot about you, but I know she had your picture on her bunk the whole time," Crystal said, smiling brightly. "That and she talked to you all the time."

"She's kinda fond of me," Shenin said, winking at Tyler.

"Do tell," Crystal said, smiling too.

Tyler went on to introduce her parents, Sheila and Jean to Crystal. There were other introductions and rounds of congratulations. At one point, Jean excused herself from the group. When she returned she had no less than a two-star general in tow. Everyone in the vicinity snapped to attention and saluted immediately. The general returned the salute; Sheila was glowering at Jean behind his back.

"This is my dad," Jean said. "Major General Robert McClain. Dad this is Tyler Hancock, the one who saved my life in Iraq."

"And I've been wanting to thank you for that, but Jeanie wouldn't let me," the general said, extending his hand to Tyler.

Tyler shook his hand, her eyes skipping to Jean and then back to the general, "Thank you sir," she said, smiling. "But you really don't need to, at the very least I was just doing my job; at best I was looking out for my friend."

The general nodded. "Good answer soldier," he said, grinning.

Later Jean was grilled extensively as to why she never let on that she was a general's daughter. She laughed saying that she didn't want friends that wanted to be friends with a general's daughter, she wanted real friends. Everyone accepted that answer easily enough.

They all had dinner that evening, celebrating Tyler's graduation. The next morning Sheila and Jean caught a transport back to Nellis. Tyler and Shenin took Carl and Becky to the airport. As they got ready to board their flight, Shenin hugged them both, then stepped aside to give Tyler privacy to say goodbye to her parents. Tyler hugged them both.

"Thank you for coming," Tyler said to them.

"We are really proud of you," Becky told her.

Tyler nodded, looking like she wanted to cry.

"We love you," Carl told her, looking into his daughter's eyes, that were so much like his own. "And I am so happy to see you happy."

Tyler nodded, the tears in her eyes now dropping as she hugged her father.

Carl and Becky left a little while later. Tyler and Shenin made their way over to the gate they were leaving from. They were flying to Sacramento that afternoon.

They got into Sacramento and picked up a rental car. As they drove away from the airport, Shenin gestured to the fields they were passing as they headed towards downtown.

"Welcome to Sacramento," she said, making a face.

"Stop it," Tyler said, grinning at her.

"It's a pit," Shenin said, "I hate Sacramento, why do you think I joined the Air Force?"

"And got stationed at Beale," Tyler put in.

"My mom was sick when I got out of basic," Shenin said. "So I got them to place me there. But once she got better, I let them reassign me."

Tyler nodded. "And lucky for me, you got assigned to Nellis."

"Lucky for you, huh?"

"Mmmhmm," Tyler said, grinning.

Within a few minutes they were nearing downtown and Shenin was pointing out Old Sacramento. "That's where the city originally started, and it kept flooding because of the river, so they had to raise all of the buildings. There's a tour about it if you want to go," she said, smiling as Tyler looked fascinated. "It's not quite the history you have back in Washington, D.C."

"Doesn't make it less interesting," Tyler said.

When they arrived at Shenin's mother's house, Tyler was surprised by the house, it was very ornate.

"It's a Victorian," Shenin said. "My mom was bound and determined to get one, it was her dream. This one was a fixer-upper, but my brother's really handy so he helped her."

"It's beautiful," Tyler said, admiring the detailing on the front of the house and the bay style windows. The front door of the house was on the second floor with a steep set of steps leading up to it.

As they got the bags out of the trunk of the car, Shenin's mother came out of the house and down the stairs. Tyler saw the similarities between Shenin and her mother instantly, right down to the red hair.

Shenin hugged her mother warmly, then turned to introduce Tyler.

"Ty, this is my mom, Trish," Shenin said, smiling.

Tyler extended her hand to the other woman, but Trish just laughed, and leaned into to hug Tyler warmly. When Trish released her, she said, "We're huggers in this family."

"Got it," Tyler said, nodding and smiling too.

"Well, come on in," Trish said, picking up one of the suitcases.

"I got it, ma'am," Tyler said, gently taking the suitcase from Shenin's mother.

Trish looked back at Tyler, then glanced at Shenin, who was smiling widely. "Told you mom, she's gallant."

"I guess so," Trish said, unhanding the suitcase and reaching for a smaller carryon bag. "This okay?" she asked Tyler, her smile teasing.

"I suppose," Tyler said, her grin teasing as well.

Tyler gestured for Shenin and her mother to precede her, and Trish chuckled shaking her head, as she lead the way to the house.

"Tyler, be careful on these steps, they're really steep," she cautioned.

"Yes ma'am," Tyler responded.

"And stop calling me ma'am," Trish said. "I'm either Mom or Trish, take your pick."

Shenin grinned to herself, knowing that Tyler and her mom were bound to go a few rounds with how formal and polite Tyler was, versus how casual her mom was with people. It was bound to be amusing.

"Shenin, I put you and Tyler in the blue room," Trish was saying. "Your old room was too small for a decent sized bed. The blue room has a queen," she said, shocking the hell out of Tyler by winking at her.

A few minutes later in the room they were staying in Tyler commented on it.

"She's totally okay with this, isn't she?" Tyler asked, having expected some level of weird with Shenin's mother. After all, her daughter left Sacramento as a straight woman and was now returning with her girlfriend.

"My mom doesn't care who I'm with, whether it's a man or a woman, as long as they make me happy. And she knows how happy you make me."

Tyler nodded, looking like she was having trouble believing that.

"Ty," Shenin said, touching her hand, "she's the one who informed me that you were in love with me. In fact, she pointed out the fact that I was in love with you too."

Tyler looked shocked. "Really?"

"Yep," Shenin said, nodding. "When I was here after OTS. She knew I missed you terribly, and that it was making me miserable."

Tyler pressed her lips together in chagrin. "Yeah, that time sucked for both of us."

Shenin nodded. "Come on," she said, "I know Mom's gonna want to give you the tour. This house is her pride and joy, besides me and Steve of course."

“Of course,” Tyler said, grinning.

CHAPTER 12

Shenin was right; Trish gave Tyler a whole tour of the house, ending up in Trish's own bedroom done in bright purples and blues. There were many pictures on her wall, and Tyler became engrossed in looking at them. They were all pictures of Shenin and her brother Steve, but mostly of Shenin. There were pictures of her in formal wear like proms, but also candid pictures of holidays, opening presents or toasting, or just laughing or smiling at the camera, also many pictures where she was sticking her tongue out. Tyler noticed that many of the pictures featured guys next to her smiling. And she also noticed that there weren't many pictures of the same guy. She asked Shenin about it later that night.

They were lying in bed, Tyler was lying on her back, and Shenin lay beside her on her side, looking down at her.

"So," Tyler said.

"A needle pulling thread," Shenin replied, grinning.

"Smart ass," Tyler countered.

"And?" Shenin said, "oh, wait, was that your point?"

Tyler chuckled. "Definitely."

"Lame point," Shenin said, leaning down to kiss her lips.

"Anyway," Tyler said, grinning, "exactly how many men did you date back here?"

Shenin looked back at her for a minute, her look considering. "I had a lot of short-term relationships," she said, her tone making Tyler narrow her eyes.

"What does that mean?" she asked.

Shenin blew her breath out, which told Tyler that she was about to hear something she didn't like.

"There were a lot of issues back then," Shenin said.

"Issues?" Tyler asked, smoothing her hand across Shenin's back, trying unconsciously to soothe the turbulent look in Shenin's eyes.

"With sex," Shenin said so simply it took Tyler a second to catch up.

"Wait," Tyler said, her voice cautious, "in terms of what?"

"In terms of the fact that I didn't always give it up," Shenin said, her tone hurried, like she was trying to get through the subject quickly.

Tyler looked back at her for a moment, looking confused, and then understanding started to dawn. "And how did that go?" she asked, sensing the seriousness of the conversation suddenly.

Shenin looked away, staring at a spot on the wall. "Not always great," she said. "It would always start out great. The guy was nice, he was polite. Then after a few times when we'd make out, he'd make his big move, and I'd put him off. A lot of times, he'd be annoyed, but chalk it up to me playing hard to get."

Tyler closed her eyes, knowing what was coming next. Her hand at Shenin's waist tightened, as she turned on her side to face her.

"And when he still didn't get in there, sometimes..." Shenin said, her voice trailing off as she looked at Tyler. "Let's just say that the Dan thing wasn't the first time that happened to me."

"Oh my God..." Tyler said, her voice devastated for the woman she loved, "Shen," she said, as she pulled her into her arms, hugging her close.

They stayed that way for a while, Shenin taking comfort in the arms that had always made her feel safe from everything, and Tyler trying to wrestle with the need to hit some stupid man.

"I guess," Shenin said, moving to look at Tyler, "it explains why this," she said, gesturing between them, "feels so natural, when that didn't."

Tyler looked considering, then nodded. "Could be," she said, reaching her hand up to smooth her thumb over Shenin's forehead gently, like she was trying to erase the memory of the bad experiences.

"Men suck," Shenin said, making a face.

"Well, yeah, that's why I don't date them," Tyler replied, grinning.

Shenin chuckled. "And I thought it was because you're gay."

"Oh, well, that too," Tyler said. "So, you think any of those guys are still around?" she asked, the look in her eyes malicious.

"Tyler," Shenin cautioned. "You are an Air Force officer now, and that was a long time ago."

Tyler curled her lips in disgust. "Doesn't keep me from wanting to beat some male ass right now."

Shenin nodded, feeling a sense of awe that Tyler was so protective; she loved it, and the woman that felt it about her.

The next day, they went to Old Sacramento and walked along the planked boardwalk. They spent time wandering through the many shops, even stopping for ice cream in one store. They managed to get a tour of the "tunnels" and learned more about how the buildings were raised in that part of town due to seasonal flooding. They had lunch on an old paddleboat that was docked in the river called the Delta King. It was a nice day.

That night they had dinner with Shenin's older brother. Tyler was not surprised by Shenin's brother, he was a good looking, outgoing kind of person. He greeted Tyler warmly and seemed to have no problem with the gay thing at all.

"Guess that's why it never worked out with Mark, huh?" Steve said to Shenin, winking at her.

"Yeah," Shenin said, not smiling, "that's probably it."

Tyler's head came up slightly as she heard the tone, and she looked at Shenin. Shenin's eyes connected with hers for a long moment, and Tyler knew that this was one of the guys that hadn't wanted to take no for an answer.

"You still friends with this Mark?" Tyler asked, her tone completely conversational.

"Oh yeah," Steve said, nodding. "He's my wingman," he said grinning.

Tyler narrowed her eyes slightly. "Interesting," she commented simply.

Shenin looked over and Tyler and knew that there was trouble brewing there, she just hoped that they'd be lucky enough not to see Mark while they were in town.

It was too much to hope for though, because the very next day, Mark found it necessary to show up at the house. Steve had told him that Shenin was in town. What he'd failed to tell Mark was that Shenin was dating someone and that someone was a woman.

Shenin and Tyler were sitting on the back porch when the door opened and a man stepped out on the porch. He was a couple of inches taller than Tyler, and he looked like the all-American football hero, with brown eyes and blond hair. Tyler hated him on sight.

Shenin jumped up quickly, putting herself between the man and Tyler. Tyler knew then that this had to be Mark. She moved to stand.

"Mark," Shenin said, her tone surprised, "what are you doing here?"

She could feel Tyler's tension from behind her, and was hoping to avoid a nasty confrontation. She thought that if Mark was just smart enough not to push his luck. Smart wasn't really Mark's forte though.

Mark moved forward, taking Shenin in his arms and hugging her, his eyes looking behind her to the woman standing there. It was obvious he didn't know who Tyler was.

"Steve told me you were here," he said, with a smile. "I missed you last time you were here, so I wanted to come by and see ya this time." His eyes strayed over to Tyler again.

"Oh," Shenin said, "Mark, this is Tyler."

Mark stepped forward, putting his hand out to Tyler, curiosity in his eyes. Tyler took his hand firmly, shaking it as her blue eyes stared directly back into his, a glint of malice there.

"So how do you know, Shenin?" Mark asked Tyler, his curiosity getting the better of him.

Tyler didn't answer for a moment, allowing a smirk to appear.

"We're in the Air Force together," Shenin put in, not sure if she could diffuse this bomb before it went off or not.

"Oh," Mark said, nodding, looking like he was relieved and chiding himself for thinking something else. Tyler couldn't let that stand.

"And we're dating," Tyler said, her tone informative with just an edge to it, but Shenin was the only one that heard that.

Mark's mouth literally dropped open in shock, and he actually backed up a step too. Suddenly he recognized that malicious glint in Tyler's eyes, which only served to increase Tyler's ire.

"I…" Mark stammered, looking from Tyler to Shenin. "Well, I…" he continued, "that's interesting."

"Is it?" Tyler asked, her tone quizzical.

"Well, yeah," Mark said, his voice still halting, "I mean, she always," he began, but then realized what he was about to say and clamped his mouth shut.

Shenin grimaced, knowing what he'd been about to say, and sensing the increased tension from behind her, she knew Tyler did too.

"She was always what?" Tyler asked, her tone dropping a dangerous octave.

Mark looked taken aback by the threat in Tyler's voice. It irritated him.

"She was always kinda cold, ya know?" he said, trying to play it off.

"Cold?" Tyler repeated, her eyes sparkling.

"Yeah, you know, like not into it?" Mark said, trying to pull the 'it was her, not me' thing.

"Maybe it was just the way you did it," Tyler said.

"What's that mean?" Mark replied.

"Not all women like to be forced if they don't give in," Tyler said.

Mark took a menacing step forward, his look at Shenin shocked. Tyler put her arm around Shenin's waist, pulling her back against her chest, her look at Mark warning.

"You even think about putting your hands on her, I'll take them off for you," Tyler told him, her tone all Security Force now.

"You think you could take me?" Mark said, his tone snide.

"I think I'd like to find out," Tyler countered.

"Wait, wait!" Shenin said, turning in Tyler's arms and looking up at her. "Babe, he's really not worth it," she said. "It was a long time ago, lieutenant," she said, emphasizing Tyler's new rank.

Tyler narrowed her eyes at Shenin as she took a deep breath, blowing it out slowly. "But it would feel so good," she said, her tone matter of fact.

"I know, and he really deserves it," Shenin said, grinning, sensing Mark's ego puffing up behind her. "But do you really want to go to your next post with a sore hand?"

Tyler looked like she was considering the idea, when Mark made a big mistake.

"Fuckin' lesbos," he muttered.

That had Shenin wheeling around and punching him in the face. To Shenin's credit, Mark fell back a couple of steps, but then he narrowed his eyes and Tyler knew it was about to get nasty. Grabbing Shenin and pushing her behind her, Tyler stepped into Mark's path, but since she had Shenin behind her, she couldn't step out of the way this time. So she let him catch her in the mid-section, but she steeled for it, and was ready so he didn't actually manage to knock her down as he expected. Instead, Tyler had him in a headlock instantly, and she twisted around using his weight against him, to flip him over her back. He landed on the porch floor. Going down to her knee, she grabbed him by the throat and brought her fist up, her look deadly.

"You want to stop now," Tyler growled, "or do you need me to beat the living shit out of you?"

Mark struggled against her hold, but he didn't get very far as Tyler pressed her other knee into his chest. "You really don't want to piss me off," she said.

Trish came running out onto the porch at that point.

"What in God's name is going on – oh!" she said, suddenly seeing the scene before her.

"Mom," Shenin said, holding up her hand, "it's okay."

Tyler looked up at Trish, and Trish could see the fury still burning in Tyler's eyes, she was surprised. She then looked down at Mark, her look sympathetic.

"Mark, honey," Trish said, her tone sweet, "I guess Steve didn't tell you that Shenin and her partner were part of the security force in the Air Force. They're both kind of kick ass. So whatever you said to piss Lieutenant Hancock off, I would suggest you apologize, because honestly I don't want to have to clean blood off my porch."

Shenin couldn't hold back the laugh, and Tyler even found herself grinning. Mark, on the other hand, was mortified. Finally, he held his arms out to his sides in surrender. Tyler got up, and stepped back to allow him to scramble up off the floor.

"I think you might want to leave," Trish said to him. He nodded and headed back into the house without looking at any of them.

The three women had a good chuckle over it, but then Trish saw Shenin's hand, even as Tyler reached for it to examine it.

"Oh honey," Trish said, stepping over to look at Shenin's hand too.

Tyler looked at Shenin. "Thought we were avoiding sore hands today," she said, grinning.

"He pissed me off," Shenin said, her eyes narrowed.

Tyler nodded. "I can see that, babe," she said. "You're gonna need to put ice on this."

"What in God's name did he say?" Trish asked, sounding shocked.

"He called us 'fucking lesbos,' " Shenin said.

"Well that was rude," Trish said.

Tyler and Shenin looked at each other grinning at how simple it was for Shenin's mom to accept what she'd just seen.

They found out later at dinner that Trish had never completely liked Mark.

"He had that Eddie Haskell vibe for me," she said, making a face. "There was just something sleazy about him, like your stepfather," she said, looking at Shenin.

"That's pretty sleazy," Shenin said, glancing at Tyler with a look she didn't understand. She changed the subject right after that. It was something Tyler noted and questioned her about later.

"So, you had a stepfather?" Tyler asked curiously.

Shenin nodded, moving to turn over, putting her back to Tyler. That was yet another warning sign that Tyler recognized.

"You've never said anything about him," Tyler said, sensing it was more than just something Shenin forgot to mention. Considering the last thing she forgot to tell her about, Tyler was on high alert.

Shenin shrugged. "He was only around for a few years."

"But he was sleazy?" Tyler asked, her tone more gentle.

Shenin heard the change in Tyler's tone, and it was more than she could handle right then. Inexplicably the tears started.

"Shen?" Tyler queried, trying to get Shenin to turn back over, but she wouldn't, so Tyler got out of bed and walked around to the other side, kneeling down in front of her. Shenin squeezed her eyes shut, shaking her head.

"Babe," Tyler said, reaching out to touch her face, "please talk to me."

Shenin only cried harder. Finally, Tyler stood up, scooping her up off the bed and lying down to hold Shenin against her. She lay that way for what seemed like hours, just letting Shenin cry and get out whatever she needed to get out.

"Can you talk to me yet?" Tyler asked gently after a while.

Shenin took a deep breath, blowing it out loudly. "I'm just wondering," she said, her tone hesitant.

"Wondering what, babe?" Tyler asked when she didn't continue.

"How long it's going to take for you to get sick of dealing with all my fucking issues." Shenin said, with more venom then Tyler had ever heard from her.

"Shenin," Tyler said, looking down at her. "Everyone has issues."

"This many?" Shenin asked, sounding doubtful.

"I don't even know what issue we're talking about at this point, babe..." Tyler said, her tone beseeching.

Shenin swallowed hard. "It's really not a big leap, Ty," she said, her tone tired. "Sleazy stepfather, young girl home alone with him a lot because he didn't always have a job..."

Tyler was sure she was going to be sick as what Shenin was saying sunk in. "Oh my God, Shen..." she said, not even sure what she could say at this point to try to make things better.

"I'm a broken mess," Shenin said matter-of-factly.

"And I love you," Tyler said, kissing her forehead.

"You love broken messes?" Shenin asked, sniffling.

"Just one," Tyler said, grinning.

"That's me, right?" Shenin said, sounding very young at that moment.

"Yes, that's you," Tyler said, hugging her closer.

"Okay," Shenin said, simply.

"Good," Tyler replied.

They fell asleep that night just like that.

The next day, when she woke, Tyler saw that Shenin was already awake and watching her sleep.

"Hi," she said, smiling and leaning in to kiss her.

"Hi," Shenin replied. "Look, I'm sorry about last night," she said, it was obvious she'd been stewing on it for a while, so Tyler just let her talk. "I've spent a lot of time trying to pretend that none of that happened, and sometimes it really just catches up on me. That's what happened last night, I just couldn't really take that along with what happened with Mark, it was just too much."

Tyler took a deep breath, feeling a stab of guilt, moving to sit up, she looked at Shenin, "Well, I didn't need to nail you with that last night, either, so I'm sorry too."

"You couldn't have known," Shenin said.

"No, but I figured it probably wasn't something simple, by the way you changed the subject. I could have just let it go," Tyler said, feeling like a louse all of a sudden.

"Ty," Shenin said, smiling because no matter what, the woman just took on everything. "It's okay, really. It's something that I've never really dealt with, so it's just an unhealed wound sitting in there, you couldn't have even imagined that one."

Tyler nodded, willing to accept that she wasn't completely at fault in this case. "You have more reason to hate men, than most lesbians do," Tyler observed.

Shenin grinned. "Yeah, probably, huh?"

"So I guess that theory you had about women being made into lesbians by lousy men in their life wasn't just a theory, huh?"

"Nope," Shenin said, "but I don't think I really realized that I was totally talking about myself at the time."

Tyler nodded. "I get that."

That day, Tyler and Shenin were on their way to San Francisco, Shenin was driving since she knew the way. Tyler was checking her emails when she saw one from the Air Force. She opened it and read the contents.

"Son of a bitch..." Tyler muttered.

"What?" Shenin asked, glancing over at her.

"Just got my assignment," Tyler said, not looking happy in the least.

"Okay..." Shenin said.

Tyler looked over at her, really not wanting to say it, because that would make it real.

"Tyler!" Shenin practically shouted, "tell me!"

Tyler blew her breath out. "I got Andrews,"

Shenin looked over at Tyler, "Seriously?" she asked, seeing the irony in the whole thing.

Tyler had been requesting Andrews for years, and now that she wanted to go somewhere else, she'd been assigned to Andrews Air Force Base in Washington, D.C.

"I fucking hate the Air Force," Tyler said, shaking her head.

"No, you don't," Shenin said. "They are just a little behind the times here," she said, grinning. "I mean you did want Andrews."

"Last time! Last time!" Tyler said. "Damnit!"

Shenin laughed. "I know."

"Damnit," Tyler repeated.

"When do you have to report?" Shenin asked.

"Four days," Tyler replied.

"Okay," Shenin said, thinking that they still had a couple of days at least. "You'll probably want to get there early."

"Bullshit," Tyler snapped, "I'll get there at the last fucking minute."

Shenin took a deep breath, knowing that Tyler was stressing, so the last thing she wanted to do was stress her out more. Looking around her on the road, she and made her way over to the nearest freeway exit. She pulled off on the Vallejo rest stop. Turning off the car, she turned to Tyler.

"Ty," Shenin said, her tone consoling. "It isn't all bad. I mean, you'll be near your family, and that's what you really wanted all this time, right?"

Tyler looked at her for a long moment. "No, what I really wanted was to be stationed with you. I put Eielson or Elmendorf in Alaska. I listed Fairchild or McChord in Washington State, I even listed staying at Nellis and instead they gave me fucking Andrews now!"

"Look, I have like six months left before I can request a transfer. In the meantime we'll talk all the time, and email and whatever."

"Uh-huh," Tyler said, "and what if you don't get Andrews when you request a transfer? We both know that the odds of you getting a transfer there is slim to none."

"Tyler," Shenin said, taking her girlfriend's hands. "We have to take things one step at a time, okay?"

Tyler nodded, knowing that she was just reacting to the disappointment of not getting Alaska. The last thing she wanted, though, was to ruin the rest of her time with Shenin. Leaning in she kissed Shenin, and hugged her.

"Let's go," she said, gesturing forward toward San Francisco.

They spent the day there checking out the Wharf, going to Ghirardelli square and riding the cable cars. That night they went to the Castro, an area in San Francisco that is predominantly gay.

"See?" Shenin said, pointing to a trash can with a rainbow flag on it. "They literally put a rainbow flag on anything that will stand still long enough."

Tyler grinned, it was kind of cool in her book. They had a few drinks at one of the bars, and danced a bit. At the last minute, they decided to stay in "the city" that night and rented a hotel room. For the first time since they'd been in California they made love and fell into a happy sated sleep.

When Shenin woke the next morning, Tyler wasn't in bed. Looking around, she saw Tyler standing by the window of the room looking out over the city. She was wearing her jeans from the day before, and her bra, Shenin found herself staring. This was an amazing looking woman she was in love with, all lean muscle with just a little bit of a curve where curves belonged.

"Hey," Shenin said softly.

When Tyler turned, Shenin could immediately see the seriousness on her face.

"What's going on?" Shenin asked, moving to sit up, and pulling a pillow on her lap, a subconsciously defensive gesture, Tyler saw it and it pricked her conscience.

Tyler looked at Shenin for a long minute, considering which of the thoughts she'd just been having she wanted to share. She'd awoken early, watching Shenin sleep for almost an hour, wishing things were different and wishing that she could change things, it was as frustrating as Hell.

Blowing her breath out in a deep sigh, she walked over to the bed to sit down facing Shenin.

"I just don't know what to do here," she said, honestly.

"About?" Shenin asked, sure she already knew, but wanting to be clear.

"Us," Tyler said, simply.

"What about us, Ty?" Shenin asked, no anger in her voice, her eyes searching Tyler's.

"This whole thing, me getting stationed across the country, the chances that we'll ever get to be together is getting smaller by the minute." The anger and frustration Tyler was feeling spilled out in her words, and Shenin had to force herself not to respond to the tone, because she did understand Tyler's feelings on this.

Shenin nodded. "Okay," she said, "so what are you thinking you want to do about that?" she asked, her gold eyes shining in the morning light, making it difficult for Tyler to concentrate on this conversation.

Tyler gave Shenin a somewhat stern look, sensing that Shenin was already suspecting what was coming and arming herself against it.

"I just think that maybe we should take what we've had, and..."

"No," Shenin said, interrupting her statement, there was no anger in her tone at all, it was very matter of fact.

"Shenin," Tyler began, trying to reason.

"No, Tyler, that's not an option," Shenin said, with the calmest, clearest tone and a perfectly calm look in her eyes.

Tyler narrowed her eyes at her girlfriend, on one hand annoyed that she wasn't listening to the reasons she had for what she was saying, but also warmed by the fact that Shenin wasn't ready to throw in the towel yet. Most women would have high tailed it for the door a long time ago, at least in Tyler's experience.

"Will you just listen to me?" Tyler asked, trying to keep the frustration out of her voice.

Shenin leaned back against the headboard of the bed, crossing her arms in front of the pillow on her lap, her gold eyes glittering with tolerance. "Sure," she murmured.

Tyler threw her another stern look, but found herself grinning too.

"Look, things aren't going to get easier being three thousand miles away from each other," Tyler began.

"It's more like four thousand, but who's counting," Shenin interjected with a smile.

"Four thousand miles away from each other," Tyler corrected. "It's going to be impossible to see each other, our phone bills are going to be insane, and it's just not going to work."

"How do you know?" Shenin asked, her voice calm.

"I just do," Tyler said, refusing to be dissuaded easily.

"How?" Shenin asked again.

"Shenin..." Tyler began, her voice trailing off to indicate that she was being difficult.

"Tyler," Shenin countered, "I can do this all day, if that's what you want to do, but you are not going to win this argument."

Tyler's jaw tightened, a sign that she was getting annoyed, Shenin didn't care, this was way too important to let Tyler off easy.

"And if I just break it off here and now?" Tyler countered, letting her temper get the better of her for a minute.

Shenin looked back at her passively. "Is that what you're planning to do?"

Tyler didn't answer at first. "Is that what you're going to make me do?" she fired back finally.

"Oh, no," Shenin said, with a sarcastic chuckle in her voice. "You're not putting this one on me, sister. If you want to break this off with me, then you're on your own to do that. I'm not taking the responsibility for that."

"Goddamnit Shenin!" Tyler yelled, her blue eyes flashing. "I'm trying to fucking do the right thing here!"

"And I'm not going to fucking let you!" Shenin yelled back, her gold eyes flashing too, and her face determined.

"Why?" Tyler asked, losing all her anger in the face of Shenin's.

"Because I love you, you idiot," Shenin said, reaching out to touch Tyler's cheek, "and you love me, and you're just doing this out of some stupid sense of chivalry, and I'm not going to let you do it."

Tyler closed her eyes, feeling tears sting the backs of them. Opening her eyes, she looked back at Shenin. "Are you ever going to give up on this idea of me being gallant?"

"Nope," Shenin said simply, a smile playing around the edges of her lips, "are you ever going to give up trying to protect me from things you can't control?"

"Nope," Tyler said, shaking her head.

"Then we're kind of stuck with each other, babe," Shenin told her.

Tyler sighed loudly, then she grinned. "Kinda like me, huh?"

"Lil' bit," Shenin responded.

"Lil' bit," Tyler repeated.

Tyler leaned forward, pulling the pillow out of Shenin's arms and dropping it on the floor, then pulled Shenin into her arms to hug her.

"You suck at fighting, you know?" Tyler told her.

"I suck at fighting with you," Shenin corrected.

Tyler smiled, nodding. "Okay, I'll accept that distinction."

"Good," Shenin said, giving her a dirty look.

They were both quiet for a few minutes, then Shenin looked up at Tyler.

"You really expected that to work, didn't you?" She asked, her voice soft.

"What?" Tyler asked.

"Yelling at me, to get me going, threatening me," Shenin replied.

Tyler looked circumspect. "Yeah, I did."

Shenin nodded, accepting that. "Has it worked before? On other women?"

"I usually don't wait for their permission to break up with them," Tyler said.

"I see," Shenin said, "but did they argue better?"

Tyler looked back at her, looking like she was trying to figure out where Shenin's mind was going on this, then she gave up, the woman was hard to read sometimes.

"I don't know that I'd say better," Tyler said, moving to settle against the headboard of the bed, still holding Shenin in her arms. "I'd say very differently."

"Explain that," Shenin said.

"Uh," Tyler said, looking a bit embarrassed. "Tears, screaming, name calling, sometimes flying fingernails."

"Yikes," Shenin said, at the last. "Yeah, I guess that would be different."

"No one's ever fought me on my level before," Tyler told her honestly.

Shenin nodded again. "And that's what you think I did?"

Tyler narrowed her eyes. "It isn't?" she asked.

"I'd like to think that I diffused you," Shenin said.

Tyler considered that thought. "Hmm," she murmured, "I can see that," she said, nodding.

"Still think I suck at arguing?" Shenin asked with a grin.

Tyler smiled widely. "Brat," she said simply.

"Yes ma'am," Shenin agreed.

CHAPTER 13

Leaving Sacramento was the hardest thing Tyler had ever done. Shenin was flying back to Alaska, and she was leaving for Andrews. They were both picking up transports from Travis Air Force Base. Shenin's was first to leave, so Tyler walked her to her flight, carrying her bags for her. When they got to the flight line, Tyler put the bags down and took Shenin into her arms. It was still an amazing feeling to know that no one could say anything at all about them now. Not only was Don't Ask, Don't Tell gone, but now they were both officers, and could therefore date with no fear of repercussions. It was an awesome feeling.

They kissed, making sure not to overdo it, since they were both wearing their BDUs and their officer insignias.

"Call me when you get settled at Andrews," Shenin said, looking up at Tyler.

"I will," Tyler said, nodding.

"I love you," Shenin said, "and I'm so proud of you, lieutenant."

"I love you, lieutenant," Tyler replied, grinning.

Tyler picked up Shenin's bags and walked them over to the airman putting them on the transport. The airman immediately snapped to attention and saluted Tyler, she returned the salute not sure if she was ever going to get used that people saluting her. She turned and saw Shenin watching her from the stairs grinning. Tyler winked at her, and then turned and walked away.

Andrews Air Force Base, technically known as Joint Base Andrews, was definitely an impressive base. Tyler found herself in awe of the place. She met with her commanding officer who could barely spare the time. He told her he was assigning her to the 811th Security Forces Squadron; she was to be part of the protective services branch. This was a very big surprise to her, as this particular unit actually protected the President of the United States when he was on the base. It was an unexpected assignment, and while the CO didn't expand upon exactly why she was being assigned such an honor, he did sight her excellent work in the commission of her duties.

Later in the officers' quarters, Tyler called Shenin.

"So, how is it going?" Shenin asked.

"Uh, surprising," Tyler said.

"Okay," Shenin said. "Would you like to explain that?" she asked, smiling on her end.

"Well, I got assigned to the detail that will protect Obama when he's on base," Tyler said, her tone so conversational it took Shenin a minute to catch up.

"Oh my God, did you just say that you'd be protecting our president?" Shenin asked.

"Yes, yes, that is what I said," Tyler said, grinning.

"Wow..." Shenin said, "scared of you."

"I keep waiting for them to call me back and say, 'Oh wait, we didn't mean you,' " Tyler said.

"Stop it, you're an awesome soldier, Ty, they just figured that out. Hell, maybe that's why you got assigned to Andrews in the first place."

That's when something occurred to Tyler. "That little shit..." she muttered.

"What?" Shenin asked, not having any idea what Tyler was talking about.

"Jean," Tyler said, "I will bet you serious money that Jean told her father that I should be assigned to this detail. This is his 'thank you' for saving her life."

"Wow," Shenin said. "Well, you saved Jean's life, maybe they figure you'd be good to save Obama's life too."

"Crazy," Tyler said. "How are things there?" Tyler asked.

"Snowing, again," Shenin said, sighing.

"Miss Vegas now, don't ya?" Tyler said, grinning.

"No," Shenin said, "my girl's not there anymore."

"I see," Tyler said.

"So how's the weather there?" Shenin asked.

"Cold, but not snowing at this point," Tyler answered.

The next day, Tyler's squad got their first impression of their new lieutenant. She rode up on a Harley Davidson; it had been shipped from Vegas, thanks to Jean and Sheila. She got off the bike, and walked up to the squad who were standing around until someone called them to attention.

"Ten Hut!" someone yelled, and everyone came to attention and saluted her.

Tyler shook her head in disbelief, still unreal in her head, she returned their salute and immediately called, "At ease."

"Let's head in," she said. "I'm still adjusting to the temperature change," she told them all, grinning.

Inside the squad room, she looked at her crew. There were a couple of men in there that were definitely older than her. Not sure how she was going to deal with this, she started with what she thought was logical.

"Let me start by saying that I have ten years security force training, before I became an officer. So, yeah, I'm an officer and a college graduate, but I'm not one of those college pukes that you're probably used to."

She immediately saw a lot of grins appear on faces.

"Before I went to OTS, I was stationed in Iraq, helping to shut down Joint Base Balad. I was injured by an IED and spent three months recovering after three surgeries. So I've seen action, I've seen peace, I've seen a lot. This is gonna be a whole new adventure for me, but don't think for a second that I'm new at this." Her eyes touched on each member of her new team. "I will work to earn your respect, but I do think I deserve at least a certain level solely on my experience. I will give you the respect you deserve, and I ask for one thing from all of you." She once again looked at each of them. "If you fuck up, and you will fuck up, everyone does, I want to know about it from you, before I hear about it from my boss. Is that in any way unclear?"

Everyone shook their heads.

"Good!" Tyler said. "Now, let's talk about current assignments and we'll take it from there. Sound good?"

"Yes ma'am!" came the yell from a number of Airmen.

By the end of the day, Tyler found that she had a lot of good people, and only a couple of young ones that might need a little bit work, but all in all she had a good team here.

Over the next few months Tyler found herself extremely busy. She called Shenin as often as she could, but it wasn't much as she'd like. Shenin found herself equally busy with some new work that was being done at Eielson, requiring a lot of her team's time. Regardless, she was ever hopeful that at the end of the six months, she'd get the good news that she was being reassigned to Andrews Air Force base and she could be with Tyler again.

They spent long hours on the phone, talking about what they could do when Shenin got there. There were discussions about getting a house off base, something they could fix up and live in together. The discussions were always in the vein of when the transfer came through, not "if" the transfer came through. Shenin even made a point of talking to her team about what a transition would look like when she got her transfer. It never occurred to her that it wouldn't happen.

Before long, it had been six months since Tyler had reported to Andrews. Shenin filled out her transfer request paperwork, listing Andrews as one of her requests. It was another month before she received an answer. She was not happy with the answer she received. Her CO had requested she stay at Eielson, and that request had been approved.

It made Shenin sick to make that phone call.

Tyler answered her cell with her customary phrase, but Shenin couldn't even smile at that at that point.

"Shen?" Tyler queried when Shenin was silent for a moment.

"I'm here," Shenin replied quietly.

"What's wrong?" Tyler asked, immediately on alert.

"I got the answer to my transfer request today," Shenin told her.

"And it sounds like it's not good news," Tyler said, her tone somber.

"My CO requested I stay here," Shenin said, trying desperately not to cry.

"Damn," Tyler said, having hoped that maybe she was at least getting closer to Washington, D.C.

"Yeah," Shenin said, feeling so bereft at that moment, she didn't even want to talk, what could they say at that point?

"Babe…" Tyler said, worried, "you okay?"

"No," Shenin answered honestly, the tears starting. "I just can't right now, Ty, I can't…" she said, shaking her head on the other end.

Tyler closed her eyes at her end, this had been what she was afraid of all along. They hung up a couple minutes later. Tyler didn't hear from Shenin for a week, and even then the conversation was stilted. She knew she was losing Shenin, and it made her sick.

In Alaska, Shenin was doing everything she could to block out the sadness that was threatening to overwhelm her. She felt like everything was slipping away from her. The feeling of overwhelming sadness permeated everything she did, everything she felt. It didn't help that it was winter in Alaska so the days were shorter and the nights seemed like forever. The temperatures even during the day were so cold that there was no going outside unless you absolutely had to do so. It was the time of year when normally happy people had a lot of problems with what they called "cabin fever". People got to feeling like they were never going to get outside and see the sun again, and it would drive them crazy.

For Shenin it was more than that, she knew she was stuck in Alaska for at least another eighteen months, and even then, her CO could pull the same thing on her. The woman she loved more than anything was across the country. Lying in the darkness one night, Shenin started to think that it might just be easier to quit the Air Force, even so, she still had a year left on her current enlistment, so that wasn't really a solution yet either. She was starting to see no way out and entertained much darker thoughts. Caught up in those thoughts, she actually called off shift for two days.

Anne was worried; Tyler had called her and told her what was going on. Shenin hadn't answered her phone for two days and Tyler was panicking. Anne went to the house Shenin was renting and used the key Shenin had given her, when she didn't answer the door.

Anne was extremely relieved to find Shenin lying in bed.

"Hey," Anne said from the doorway.

Shenin turned over and looked at Anne, her face was pale. Anne walked over to the bed and sat down looking at her critically.

"Ty called you," Shenin said, her voice hoarse from disuse.

"She's worried about you," Anne said.

Shenin nodded numbly.

She reached into the pocket of her uniform. "She sent you this," she said, handing Shenin an envelope.

Shenin moved to sit up, taking the envelope. She opened it to find an airline ticket to Washington, D.C. and a note attached. "I love you, please come see me."

The date on the ticket was for that night.

"I'll drive you to Fairbanks," Anne said. "Now we just have to get you cleaned up and packed."

Five hours later Shenin was on a flight to Washington, D.C., she slept most of the way. She woke an hour before they landed. She went to the bathroom and did her best to clean up. She put make-up on and brushed out her hair.

When the plane landed, Shenin waded through the group getting off the plane. Finally, she walked off the plane and saw Tyler waiting at the gate. She was wearing her BDUs. When she saw Tyler, she ran to her, throwing herself into her arms.

Tyler hugged her close. "I got you babe, I got you," she said, softly.

Shenin held on to Tyler for what seemed like hours. When she finally eased her hold, Tyler looked down at her and set her back on her feet. Then to Shenin's shock, she dropped to one knee, holding up a box with a diamond ring in it.

"Marry me," Tyler said simply. "I love you, I need you, and I can't live without you."

Everyone in the terminal stood staring, there were plenty of "awwws" in the group and a few claps too.

Shenin stared at the ring, and then looked at Tyler, she dropped to her knees and hugged Tyler, nodding. "Oh my god, yes!"

"Whew," Tyler said, grinning as she put the ring on Shenin's shaking hand. Cheers went up in the airport, and Tyler and Shenin laughed and kissed.

Getting up, and pulling Shenin up with her, she took her hand to walk her to the baggage claim. By this time, Shenin had gotten her wits back. While they were waiting for her bags, she started to look pained. Tyler saw it immediately and knew what was going on in her mind. Shenin was thinking that this proposal didn't change anything for the next eighteen months.

Reaching into her inner pocket Tyler pulled out a folded sheet of paper and handed it to Shenin.

"What's this?" Shenin asked.

"Read it," Tyler said simply.

Shenin opened it and read the words on the paper, then re-read them.

"Ty," she said, sounding stunned, "this says that I'm transferred to Andrews as of tomorrow..."

"Yep," Tyler said, reaching out to grab Shenin's bag off the conveyor.

"But how?" Shenin asked.

"Apparently," Tyler said, turning to Shenin, "it pays to save the life of a Major General's daughter."

Shenin gave a scream of joy and once again launched herself into Tyler's arms, hugging her and kissing her deeply, not caring what anyone thought at that moment in time.

After a few minutes, they parted and Tyler looked down at her.

"So you kinda like me, huh?" Tyler asked.

Shenin smiled through the instant tears. "Lil' bit," she said.

Tyler reached out with her thumb and brushed away a tear.

"Lil' bit," she repeated.

EPILOGUE

The night before the wedding, Tyler and Shenin slept in separate rooms in the Georgian Style Colonial house where they were having their wedding the next day. Although neither of them was actually sleeping. Shenin padded down the hallway of the house, poking her head into the room Tyler was sleeping in, she saw that Tyler was indeed awake too.

"Hi," she said, grinning.

"Hi," Tyler replied. "Can't sleep?"

"Apparently I'm not the only one," Shenin said, grinning.

Tyler shifted on the bed, making room for Shenin.

Shenin lay down, wrapping her arm around Tyler's waist and putting her head in the hollow of Tyler's shoulder. She sighed contentedly then.

"I can't sleep alone anymore," she said, grinning.

"No?" Tyler asked, smiling as she did.

"Uh-uh," Shenin said, "I think I'm spoiled now."

They'd been together every night since Shenin had gotten there six months before. Tyler found that it was hard for her to sleep without Shenin next to her either. It wasn't a bad habit to have, she thought.

"Are you nervous about tomorrow?" Shenin asked.

"Nope," Tyler answered immediately.

"Not even a little bit?" Shenin asked.

Tyler looked down at her. "Why would I be?" she asked, her tone quizzical. "I'm marrying my very best friend who I'm madly in love with."

Shenin smiled, she loved that Tyler still said things like that and she hoped she never stopped.

"Well, that's true," Shenin said, "I am pretty damned lucky you found me, or did I find you?"

"I'd say the Air Force was kind enough to place us in each other's paths," Tyler said, amicably.

Shenin nodded. "I can accept that," she said. "But if I hadn't been a royal pain in your ass, we might still be just friends," she said, her tone chiding.

Tyler sighed. "Oh, I don't know about that," she said, grinning. "The knock down of Don't Ask, Don't Tell, helped a lot."

"So you think we would have gotten together then?" Shenin asked, curious.

"I knew I was in love with you back when you were shot," Tyler said. "Before that I suspected it, but I didn't want to see it. I don't think that once I didn't have the excuse of DADT I could have stayed away much longer."

"But there was the fraternization," Shenin pointed out.

"And you see how easily I solved that, right?" Tyler countered.

Shenin laughed. "Good point," she said. "There was still the distance thing though," she said then, her tone changing slightly.

Tyler narrowed her eyes slightly, it was something she'd wanted to talk to her about for the last six months, but there hadn't seemed to be a good time. The night before they got married, seemed like a good time.

"About that," Tyler said, gently, touching Shenin's face gently.

Shenin looked back at her, and nodded slowly. "I'm sure you know," she said, her voice soft, "what was going on with me those last couple of days in Alaska."

Tyler nodded, her look pained. "I definitely suspected," she answered. "You had me worried sick."

Shenin pressed her lips together, taking a deep breath and blowing out in a long quiet sigh. "I'm sorry, I just couldn't see how things were ever going to get better."

"Babe," Tyler said. "You gotta know that if you'd actually done anything," she said, shaking her head, "my life would have been over too."

Shenin looked back at her, her look shocked.

"You think I'd want to go on without you?" Tyler asked, the tone of her voice answering the question.

"I didn't really think of it that way," Shenin said, honestly ashamed that her near fatal weakness could have had completely unexpected consequences.

"I can't live without you," Tyler said, repeating part of what she'd said that day in the airport when she'd proposed. "I meant that, babe."

Shenin swallowed hard, nodding her head. Tyler hugged her close, hoping she'd gotten her message across. It was impossible to explain to Shenin how much she meant to her, no words would suffice, but she'd had to try.

The next day dawned a beautiful spring day. The wedding took place on the back lawn of the house that overlooked the Patuxent River. It was a small wedding with mostly family and friends. Most of Tyler's family was in attendance, and they made up the lion's share of the guests. The house they were getting married at belonged to one of Tyler's cousins. Shenin's mother and brother attended. Sheila, Jean, and Anne were all in attendance as well. Some of Tyler's staff attended, since they'd decided they really liked their lieutenant, and the woman she was marrying. As were a couple of Shenin's staff.

The ceremony was sweet and simple with Tyler and Shenin writing their vows. When it came time for the vows, the two women turned to each other taking each other's hands. Tyler wearing a well cut tuxedo, never one to be the girly girl, spoke first.

"Ever since the day I met you, you've been an important part of my life. You were there for me during the worst thing that ever happened to me and you've been there to make the best parts of my life, including today, the very best days ever. I love you more than I'll ever be able to tell you, but I plan to show you for the rest of our lives."

Shenin squeezed Tyler's hands, trying desperately not to cry.

"Tyler, ever since the day I met you, you've been rescuing me from one thing or another," Shenin said with a grin and a wink, "but you've always been in my heart. From the minute I saw you get off that Harley at the admin building, until this very day, you have been the only person for me. And from this day on, I will take your heart and protect it as my own. Thank you for giving me the chance to be so happy. I love you."

There were "awwws" and "ohhs" all around, and some quiet clapping.

"Tyler, Shenin, you may now kiss your bride," said the officiate.

Tyler leaned in, kissing Shenin's lips, pulling her close to deepen the kiss. That's when the cat calls started, and before long the two were laughing. As their lips parted, the song 'I Kissed a Girl' began with the line 'I kissed a girl and I liked it' belting out of the speakers. That pretty much said it all.

Later that night, as the party wound down, Tyler and Shenin sat on the boat dock of the house, looking out over the river. Tyler sat with her back against one of the timbers, and Shenin sat between her legs, her back pressed against Tyler's chest, her head resting against Tyler's shoulder, their hands were intertwined.

"Did you ever think we'd end up here?" Shenin asked wistfully.

"I never even dared to hope it," Tyler answered honestly.

Shenin smiled, so happy at that moment, she didn't think she could do it justice with words.

"Did you ever think you'd end up here?" Tyler asked, glancing down at Shenin.

Shenin glanced up and back at Tyler. "I never thought I could be this happy, Ty, I really didn't."

Tyler nodded. "Sometimes we don't actually know what we want, till it's in front of us," she said.

"You're right about that," Shenin said, smiling. "All it took was one hot lesbian on a Harley," she said, grinning at that last part.

"Yeah, and a feisty little redhead, who wouldn't leave my mind for a second," Tyler said.

"Kinda like me, huh?" Shenin said, grinning.

"Lil' bit," Tyler replied.

Shenin moved to sit up, turning to Tyler. "Better be a lot, babe, we're married now," she said, grinning.

"Well, if you insist," Tyler replied, taking Shenin into her arms and kissing her deeply.

Made in the USA
San Bernardino, CA
03 June 2017